TWO NO
After & Makir

Gabriel Josipovici was born in Nice in 1940 of Russo-Italian, Romano-Levantine parents. He lived in Egypt from 1945 to 1956, when he came to Britain. He read English at St Edmund Hall, Oxford, graduating with a First in 1961. From 1963 to 1996 he taught at the University of Sussex, where he is now Research Professor in the Graduate School of Humanities. He has published over a dozen novels, three volumes of short stories and a number of critical books. His plays have been performed throughout Britain and on radio in Britain, France and Germany, and his work has been translated into the major European languages and Arabic. In 2001 he published *A Life*, a biographical memoir of his mother, the translator and poet Sacha Rabinovitch (London Magazine editions). His most recent works are a collection of essays, *The Singer on the Shore* and a novel, *Everything Passes*, both published by Carcanet.

Also by Gabriel Josipovici

Fiction
The Inventory (1968)
Words (1971)
Mobius the Stripper: Stories and Short Plays (1974)
The Present (1975)
Four Stories (1977)
Migrations (1977)
The Echo Chamber (1979)
The Air We Breathe (1981)
Conversations in Another Room (1984)
Contre Jour: A Triptych after Pierre Bonnard (1987)
In the Fertile Land (1987)
Steps: Selected Fiction and Drama (1990)
The Big Glass (1991)
In a Hotel Garden (1993)
Moo Pak (1995)
Now (1998)
Goldberg: Variations (2002)
Everything Passes (2006)

Theatre
Mobius the Stripper (1974)
Vergil Dying (1977)

Non-fiction
The World and the Book (1971, 1979)
The Lessons of Modernism (1977, 1987)
Writing and the Body (1982)
The Mirror of Criticism: Selected Reviews (1983)
The Book of God: A Response to the Bible (1988, 1990)
Text and voice: Essays 1981-1991 (1992)
(ed.) *The Modern English Novel: The Reader, the Writer and the Book* (1975)
(ed.) *The Siren's Song: Selected Essays of Maurice Blanchot* (1980)
A Life (2001)
The Singer on the Shore: Essays 1991-2004 (2006)

GABRIEL JOSIPOVICI

Two Novels

After
&
Making Mistakes

CARCANET

First published in Great Britain in 2009 by
Carcanet Press Limited
Alliance House
Cross Street
Manchester M2 7AQ

A CIP catalogue record for this book is available from the British Library

ISBN 978 1 84777 003 5

The publisher acknowledges financial assistance from Arts Council England

Typeset in Monotype Centaur by XL Publishing Services, Tiverton
Printed and bound in England by SRP Ltd, Exeter

For Tamar

After

Fragments of a Recovered Memory

Everything is less than
It is.
Everything is more.

Paul Celan

I

— I flew in from New York last night, the woman in the black leather pants says.

— Did you really?

— Day flights are so much easier, the woman says. I don't know why nobody takes them. I always do.

— Really?

— The secret, the woman says, is to get into a pool as soon after your arrival as possible and spend at least an hour working out there.

— Really?

— Believe me, the woman says. I do a hell of a lot of internal flights in the States, and I always make sure I get booked into a hotel with a pool at the other end.

— Aha.

— After an hour working out in the pool, the woman says, you sleep like a log and wake up ready for anything. Believe me.

— Of course I believe you.

She looks at him for the first time, pushing the strands of black hair away from her face with long-fingered white hands.

— I'm Gilbert's stepdaughter, by the way, she says.

— Gilbert?

— Sam's half-brother.

— Oh, right. I didn't catch, with all this noise.

— What's that?

— I said I didn't catch everything you said because of all the noise.

— You won't believe this, the woman says, but it was snowing when I left New York.

— Is that so?

— What's that?

— I was just expressing surprise, Alan says.

— Surprise?

— At what you'd just told me about snow in New York.

— It wasn't on the news?

— Not the English news, he says. Not so far as I know.

— It will be, she says. It looked like it might be a big fall.

— And what do you do? he asks.

— What's that?

— I was wondering what you did. For a living, I mean.

— I work on this dictionary.

— What dictionary?

— I was doing articles for an encyclopaedia in Spain, she says, when I heard, through Gilbert, actually, that there was an opening on this dictionary in New York, so I jumped at it, naturally.

— Naturally?

— Naturally.

— You're a lexicographer?

— I've got my little corner, she says. Everything connected with religion and spirituality.

4

— But you trained as a lexicographer?

— I trained as a dancer, actually, she says. That's when we were living in Brazil. But I've always been interested in religion and spirituality. I have to write a book for Adelphi in Milan on the subject.

— Don't you find it hot in here? Alan asks.

— What's that?

— I said it's getting terribly hot in here.

— Well, with all these people, what can you expect?

— I think I need to get some water, he says. Will you excuse me?

In the kitchen he finds Ronnie Chinn, a red rose in his buttonhole, standing at the window, glass in hand, staring out into the darkening sky.

— I need some water, he says, turning on the tap in the sink and rinsing out his glass.

Ronnie Chinn does not move. — Octavio Paz died this morning, he says.

— Really? Alan says, filling his glass.

— I just heard the news, Ronnie Chinn says. On my way here.

He drains his glass and refills it. — How old was he? he asks.

— Not that old.

— He'd been ill?

— I don't know, Ronnie Chinn says. I just heard on the radio that he'd died.

— You like his work? Alan asks. He drains a second glass.

— So-so. I like his book on Lévi-Strauss.

— Really?

— You don't like him?

— He's just a name to me.

— He was in the airport in Bangkok. On his way back from a lecture tour of Australia.

— Really?

— So they said on the radio.

Ronnie Chinn rocks gently on the balls of his feet, contemplating his reflection in the window.

— How're things? Alan asks, rinsing out his glass.

— What things?

— You know. Everything.

— Terrible, Ronnie Chinn says. You know my father died three months ago.

— I know, Alan says. I'm sorry. You got my letter?

— I haven't opened any of the letters, Ronnie Chinn says. I couldn't bear to.

— Sarah found it helped. When her mother died. Answering them.

— I couldn't bear to, Ronnie Chinn says. Not any of them.

— I understand. You don't have to apologise.

Ronnie Chinn is silent, gazing out and sipping from his glass.

Finally he says: — He was born in 1922, I think.

— You don't know?

— I think I saw it on one of his books.

— You mean Paz?

— Didn't I say Paz? I just heard on the radio. On the way over here.

— Yes, I'm sorry, I thought you meant —

— I ought to go home, Ronnie Chinn says. I don't know why I came.

6

— I just dived in here for some water, Alan says. And to get out of the noise.

— I can't bear to be by myself, Ronnie Chinn says. But when I go out I find I can't bear to be with other people.

— I'm sorry. I'd love to come and see you if you felt...

— I'm not much fun at the moment, Ronnie Chinn says.

— That's not the point, Alan says. If you felt you wanted...

— Just give me a call before you come, Ronnie Chinn says. I have difficulty with unexpected visitors.

— Of course. I've been so busy recently I...

— You don't have to, Ronnie Chinn says.

— No no. I'll give you a ring.

In the hall a small group is gathered. Someone shouts his name and he turns round. A woman with pink hair, in pink pyjamas, is grinning at him. — You don't remember me, she says.

— Of course I do.

— Denise.

— Of course.

— I bet you don't know who I am.

— Yes I do. You're Denise.

— I bet you don't know who Denise is.

— How much?

— How much what?

— How much do you want to bet?

— I don't bet.

— You just said you bet I didn't know who you were.

— That was a way of speaking.

— I see.

— Who am I then?

7

— Denise.

— Denise who?

— Nancy's friend.

— You remembered? You remembered we had dinner at Nancy's?

— Of course.

— You and Sarah.

— That's what I'm saying.

— I knew your aunt Nelly.

— Of course, Alan says. I remember.

— You've been avoiding me all evening.

— I haven't!

— Yes you have. I've smiled at you a couple of times and you've ignored me.

— I'm sorry. I'm short-sighted. It's always happening to me.

— Why don't you wear glasses then?

— They make me feel dizzy.

— Dizzy? Or is it vanity?

— I mean I wear them to read or when I watch a film or drive a car, but I don't like to wear them when I'm just standing around chatting.

— That's vanity.

— No it isn't. They make me feel dizzy.

— You need to change your glasses then.

The woman in the black leather pants is standing beside them.

— Do you know Rebecca? Denise says to him.

— We were just talking.

— She's Gilbert's stepdaughter.

— Yes, she was telling me.

— She's contracted to do a book for Adelphi in Milan on

8

modern spirituality.

— Yes, she was telling me.

— So she's told you all about herself.

— I'm sure not, Alan says.

— I saw Francine yesterday, Rebecca says.

— Francine? Denise says. Where?

— In New York.

— New York?

— I've just come from there. I just flew in.

— I thought perhaps she was in London.

— She was asking after you. I said I'd probably see you tonight.

— How was she?

— Good, Rebecca says.

In the garden Alan finds Fred Little talking to a small blonde with full lips.

— Ah, Fred Little says. And how is the maestro?

— OK. And you?

— This is Cynthia, Fred Little says.

— Hullo, Cynthia.

— This is Alan.

— Hi, Cynthia says.

Fred Little puts an arm round her shoulders. — His boys are great footballers, he says.

— You don't say?

— You're interested in football? Alan asks.

— Not in the slightest, she says.

— Did you see a Croatian skied down Everest the other day? Fred Little says.

— A Croatian? Cynthia says. How did he get the skis up there in the first place?

— It was the challenge, Fred Little says. Nowadays just climbing to the top is too easy. They're taking parties of school-children up there. And old age pensioners.

— Go on! Cynthia says. Schoolchildren?

— At one point, Fred Little says, he had to swerve to avoid a corpse.

— A corpse?

— Frozen solid. The slope's thick with them, apparently. Will you excuse me? I see my loved one trying to attract my attention. I suspect she would like me to take her home to her nice warm bed.

— Have you ever wanted to climb Everest? Cynthia asks when he has gone.

— No, Alan says. And you?

— Of course not.

— Why of course?

— Do I look like the mountaineering type?

— You look as if you like getting your own way, Alan says.

— That's something else, Cynthia says.

— Tell me what you do, Alan says.

— I don't do anything, she says.

— You don't?

— No. Matt earns the money and I spend it.

— That sounds delicious, Alan says.

— It is, she says, taking a sip of her drink and licking her lips.

— And why doesn't Matt help you spend it?

— He's too busy making it.

— What a happy arrangement, he says.

— It is, she says, smiling at him.

Sam Susskind is standing beside them. He takes Alan's arm.

— I don't want to interrupt anything, he says. But there's someone I'd like you to meet.

— Of course, Cynthia says.

— What a pity, Alan says. We were just having a most interesting conversation.

— Perhaps there'll be another chance to pursue it, she says, smiling at him.

— I hope so, he says.

— You're going to like this, Sam Susskind says, propelling him through the crowd, a hand on his elbow.

— I was liking that.

— So I saw.

— Cynthia what?

— Boddy.

— How many d's?

— Two.

— Pity.

— Sam, a bearded man says as they push their way through the crowded hall, I need to talk to you.

— Later, Sam says. We have to see someone. You're really going to love this, he says as they fight their way into the living-room. Once inside, though, the crowd is not so dense. Sam ushers Alan ahead of him towards the big French windows.

A woman standing gazing into the garden or into the reflection of the room, for it is quite dark outside now and the curtains are not drawn, turns as they approach.

Sam Susskind steps back.

She smiles and raises her right hand, thumb up and index finger pointing. — Bang, bang, she says.

Alan stares at her.

She lowers her hand, smiles at him. — Schnaidaire, she says.

He doesn't move.

— Alain Schnaidaire, she says.

— You like pronouncing it like that? he asks her.

— Isn't that how it's pronounced?

— Only by you.

— Only by me?

Sam Susskind has gone. They are alone, in their corner of the room and in the ghostly room outside.

She gazes at him, still smiling. — You won't say my name? she asks.

He stares at her. Finally he says: — Is Byron here?

— So, she says. You know who I am.

He stares.

— Claude, she says. Claude Grey.

— Yes, he says.

She is silent.

— What are you doing here? he asks.

— We're friends of the Susskinds.

— I mean in London.

— Byron has been invited over. To advise. You know.

— I see. And you're here for a while?

— I hope so, she says. It depends a little on Sophie. She doesn't seem to be settling down too well at the moment.

— Sophie?

— My daughter.

— Ah.

She gazes at him, no longer smiling.

— How old is she? he asks.

— Seven. A difficult age.

— Yes.

— I see.

He examines her in the mirror of the pane.

— And you have two boys, I understand, she says. And a loving wife.

— You're well informed.

— I try to be.

He is silent.

— You don't look a day older, Alain, she says.

— Alan, he says.

— Alain to me, she says.

— But it's Alan here, he says.

— As you wish, she says.

He is silent.

— We've taken a house not far from here, she says. Holland Park.

— Very nice, he says.

— You must come to dinner. With Sarah.

— Oh, he says. Sarah, is it?

She laughs. — We must arrange it, she says.

He becomes aware, in the windows, of the room now emptying behind them. — Since when do you know the Susskinds? he asks.

— Oh, we know everybody, she says.

— How did you know we were friends?

— I asked. I ask everyone.

— Really?

— Of course.

— Why of course?

She laughs. — I don't know, she says.

He glances at his watch.

— You're in a hurry? she asks.

— It's Sarah. She hasn't been well.

— So Sam said. Nothing serious I hope?

— No no. A touch of flu. But I said I wouldn't stay long.

He puts out a hand to the book-case next to the window.
— You took me by surprise, he says.

— That was the intention.

— I see.

She watches him, smiling.

— Why? he asks at last.

— I don't know. It took my fancy.

— Ah, he says. That old fancy.

— You remember it?

— Of course.

He glances at his watch again.

She starts to laugh.

— What? he says.

— That look at the watch, she says. When you feel trapped.

— No no, he says. It's Sarah. She —

— It doesn't matter, she says. Now I'm here.

She rummages in her bag, holds something out to him. —
Here, she says.

— What is it?

— My card.

— Your card?

— You know what we Americans are like.

— But you're not American. You're French and English.

— I think I've been living there long enough to qualify, she
says. Put it in your wallet. In case you want to call me.

She watches as he does so.

— Don't lose it, she says.

— I'll try not to.

— It doesn't matter, she says. Even if you do. You won't call me anyway. But I'll call you.

— You've got my number?

— I'll get it off Sam.

— Of course.

— Perhaps we could have coffee one of these days.

— That would be lovely.

— As well as dinner, of course. But I'd like to see you on your own.

— Why?

— Why? she says. How can you ask that?

He is silent.

— Shall we fix it now? she says.

— Why don't I give you a ring? he says. I don't have my diary with me.

— Of course, she says. You're a busy man. I don't have anything to do except write my books and look after Sophie. And she's at school most of the time. You know what the headmaster said to me when I first went round with her? Mrs Grey, he said, don't expect your daughter to learn anything here. Do you know what schools here have become, Mrs Grey? he said. They have to all intents and purposes become holding centres for the older child. We consider we have done well, he said, if the children do not murder each other while they are with us. Of course I am exaggerating, Mrs Grey, he said, getting up from his desk and helping me into my coat. But not much. What I am trying to say, Mrs Grey, he said, is that you must not expect her to learn very much, except how to grow up in a city. Then he laughed and showed me out.

— You've gone to the wrong school, he says.

— It was the third one I tried, she says.

— And?

— And what? she says.

— How is it?

— The jury's still out.

He glances at his watch again.

— I know, she says. You've got to go.

— It's only that Sarah...

She smiles at him. — Don't worry, she says. If you don't call, I will. I've got you at the end of my line, so to speak.

— Ah, he says. Yes.

She is silent.

He holds out his hand. — Goodbye, he says.

— You won't kiss me?

— No, he says.

She shrugs.

— Goodbye, he says again.

— *À bientôt*, she says. Alain.

The woman in the pink pyjamas is still in the hall. — We never had our chat, she says.

— I'm sorry. I'm trying to leave.

— So early?

— It's Sarah. She isn't well.

He finds Sam Susskind in the kitchen, uncorking bottles. — I have to go, he says.

— So soon?

— It's Sarah. I feel...

Sam Susskind looks up from his bottles and stares at him. — Are you all right? he asks.

— Yes. Why?

— I don't know. You... I didn't fuck up, did I?

— What did she say about me?

— Nothing. She wanted to trace you.

— What did she say?

— She told me about Princeton.

— What did she say?

— Nothing. How she'd known you there. That sort of thing.

— Is that all?

— Is there more?

— I'm sorry. I really have to go.

— I thought it would be a nice surprise. She's quite a looker, isn't she?

— You think so?

— Not you?

Sam Susskind returns to his bottles. — I think she's sexy, he says.

— Really?

— Very, Sam Susskind says. Give Sarah my love, he says. I'm sorry she wasn't here to brighten up the proceedings.

— I will, Alan says. Thanks for the party.

— My pleasure, Sam Susskind says.

In the porch he stops to light a cigarette.

— Is that Alan? a voice says.

He peers into the darkness. — Who's that? he says.

— Ben.

— Ben! I haven't seen you for ages.

Two figures step up onto the porch. — You know Nigel, don't you? Ben says.

— Of course. I didn't see you inside.

— We stayed in the garden. It was too crowded inside.

— I never see you these days.

— I don't get up to town much, Ben says.

— When's your next show?

— What next show?

— I thought there was always a next show?

— Don't bet on it, Ben says.

— Why? Aren't you painting?

— Sure. But it's crap.

— What do you mean it's crap?

— I mean it's crap.

— Why do you paint crap?

— I don't want to paint crap. But it comes out as crap.

— He's doing wonderful work, Nigel says. Don't let him tell you otherwise.

— It's crap, Ben says.

— Only he keeps on destroying it, Nigel says. He takes pleasure in ripping it up and stamping on the pieces.

— Why? Alan asks.

— Because it's crap, Ben says.

— It's no crappier than you used to paint, Nigel says.

— It was always crap, Ben says. Only I tried not to notice.

— Other people don't think so, Nigel says.

— Other people are blind, Ben says. Look at the stuff they like. It's all crap There's only expensive crap and ridiculously expensive crap.

— And which is yours?

— Mine's just crap.

— He always talks like that, Nigel says. Don't pay any attention to him.

— Alan's got a good pair of eyes on him, Ben says. He knows crap when he sees it. Believe me.

They go down the steps and out of the little front garden into the street.

— It's all crap, Ben says. The government's crap. The media's crap. The education system's crap. The country's crap.

— Why don't you go and live abroad? Alan says.

— Abroad? Ben says. Abroad? The whole world's crap. North south east and west. And all the fucking middle.

— Now you know, Nigel says.

— It was good to see you both, Alan says, getting out his car keys.

— That your vehicle? Ben asks.

— Do you want a lift? Alan asks. Or is that crap as well?

— No, it's not crap, Ben says. It's German. They still know how to make a thing or two.

— Their artists are pretty crappy though, Nigel says.

— Don't talk to me about their artists, Ben says. Inflated Kiefer crap. Upside down Baselitz crap. Tasty tasty Richter crap. Boring boring Gorsky crap. Ugh.

— You've got my number, haven't you? Alan says, getting into his car. Give me a ring next time you're in town.

— You know how much a crappy train ticket costs these days? Ben says.

— You too, Alan says to Nigel.

— Will do, Nigel says.

— Eighteen bloody quid off-peak return, Ben says. Eighteen bloody quid *not before ten* and *not between five and seven Monday to Thursday every alternative month except for leap years.* If that isn't crap, what is?

— See you both then, Alan says, starting up the engine.

II

— It's called 'My Folk', Simon says, sipping his mug of tea. Alan stares at the canvas in silence.

— My mother, my father, my brother, my two sisters, Simon says.

— Yes, Alan says. And is that you there in the turban?

— It's not a turban. It's my working hat.

— I'm sorry.

They gaze at the canvas, sipping their mugs of tea.

— I don't know why, Simon says, but it never feels finished without me there somewhere.

— It says: This isn't how these people *are*, it's how I see them, Alan says.

— I suppose that's it, Simon says. But it isn't any intellectual thing, you know. The canvas always feels empty, no matter how crowded it is, if I'm not there somewhere, even if it's just a token me, as in that picture of the opera.

Alan steps up to the canvas and covers a portion of it with his hand. — Yes, he says. I see.

— Of course it can become a cliché like everything else,

Simon says. But I just seem to need it. The pictures need it. But me too, come to think of it. As if I'm being dishonest if I don't include it, and if I feel I'm being dishonest I simply can't proceed. Physically, I mean. It's not an intellectual thing. I just can't lift up my hand and put paint on the canvas. Funny, isn't it?

Afterwards, in the vegetarian Indian place round the corner from the studio, he says: — Of course as soon as you think it might be a cliché you're doomed.

— So you've got to repress the thought?

— I suppose so. To get anything done.

— That is the sublime and refined point of felicity, Alan says, called the possession of being well deceived. The serene and peaceful state of being a fool among knaves.

— Swift?

— Who else?

— You think those are the alternatives? Simon asks. Fool or knave?

— I think you've got to keep the knave quiet and then perhaps wisdom will emerge. Sop to Cerberus kind of thing.

— I'm not sure about wisdom, Simon says. Shall we order?

When the waiter has gone he says: — I suppose my presence in the picture is my sop to Cerberus. Sometimes, though, he says, one feels caught between the pointlessness of mere surface and the pointlessness of mere depth.

— I know what you mean, Alan says.

— I really have to force myself to keep going then, Simon says.

— Even Stravinsky had to trick himself into sitting at his desk, Alan says.

— How do you mean, trick himself?

– I don't know. It's in the conversations with Craft I think. I suppose he'd pretend he had to go into his study to get something, then pretend he had to sit at his desk to look in a drawer or something, and hey presto, there he was with nothing for it but sit down to work.

– Like Thomas Mann putting on his suit and tie and lighting the candles at the four ends of his manuscript, Simon says.

– What a prick, Alan says.

– But a good craftsman, Simon says.

Their food arrives.

– It's interesting, isn't it, Simon says, scooping rice onto his plate. It's amazing what work does. How it clears the mind. if you can force yourself past that first moment.

– Exactly, Alan says. Even my sort of work.

– You get into something and the questions sort of fall away.

– They have to be there somewhere, Alan says. But you're right. They fall away.

– It just makes me happy to make pictures, Simon says. And I know it's not a false happiness. The happiness is real all right. What else can I say?

– It's just having faith in that. Not forgetting it.

– Do you mind? Simon says, reaching across and forking a piece of okra off his friend's plate.

– Of course I mind, Alan says.

– Sorry. Sorry.

– No, I don't mind. Of course I don't.

– Sorry.

– Stop it.

– Everything all right sirs? asks the waiter.

— Delicious, Simon says. Thank you. Of course, he says, as the years pass it gets more and more difficult not to wonder if you're not perhaps hiding your head in the sand.

— You think it gets harder?

— Of course it does. Yet I feel younger and healthier now than I did at twenty. I felt terrible at twenty. I felt I was in the prime of life and bursting with energy but there was nowhere for it to go. I have less energy now but it's more contained. Channelled. I spend more time though wondering if there's any point. Not in what I'm doing but in how I'm doing it. Then we're back to the fool and the knave.

Alan gives his plate a last wipe with a piece of naan. I saw Ben last night, he says.

— Ben? Where?

— Some party.

— Anyone I know?

— The Susskinds.

— He never comes to see me, Simon says. He's never been to the studio.

— That's how he is, Alan says. You take him as he is or you leave him.

— Eight years and he's never even been to the studio, Simon says.

— He never comes to see me either, Alan says. If it's any consolation.

— We were very close once, Simon says. When we were in Hackney.

— Well, Alan says, that's Ben.

— We would talk through every problem. Every stage of every painting.

— I didn't realise you'd been that close.

— Yes, Simon says. That close. He presses his two index fingers together on the table.

— Want anything else? Alan asks, pushing his plate away.

— No no, Simon says. How was he?

— Ben?

— Uhuh.

— Grumbling about everything as usual.

— Not once in eight years, Simon says. And it isn't as if he never comes up to town. I know for a fact that he does. He stays with Frances.

— He's destroying everything he does, Alan says.

— He always did. Most of it. But he's the best of us all.

— He said it was crap.

— He always did.

— He was with Nigel.

— Nigel? Really?

— Drunk, Alan says.

— That's just his way, Simon says. Other people drink to lose their inhibitions, but he never had any in the first place. That's what I like about him.

— Do you think we basically don't change? Alan asks. That we're programmed to do certain things and keep doing them, for better or worse, till we drop?

— We think we're getting better or drying up or whatever, Simon says, but actually it's always the same, more or less.

— I don't know, Alan says. People go off. Or find something, don't they? Find their style or their subject or something. And there's ten glorious years and then they can't renew themselves and instead they start to imitate themselves.

— I suppose so, Simon says. I sometimes feel though that one never gets very good or very bad, for all one's effort. Just remains one's own mediocre self.

— That's when it's time to get back to work, Alan says.

— Yes, Simon says. Let's pay and go.

Outside, the sun is shining but the feel of autumn is in the air.

— There are two kinds of artist, Simon says as they start to walk back towards the studio. Artists like Picasso and Joyce, who think everything they do is wonderful, and artists like Giacometti and Kafka, who think everything they do is terrible. But neither is right, of course. Like everyone, artists have their ups and downs, but basically they just go on doing what they have discovered they can do and when you look back on their careers you feel both groups were wrong. A lot of what Picasso and Joyce did was mediocre and a lot of what Giacometti and Kafka did was brilliant.

— You don't think they know best?

— That's the sixty-four thousand dollar question, isn't it? Simon says. I can tell you categorically that Picasso and Joyce did not know best. Whether the other lot did is a moot point.

— You mean perhaps their work is terrible?

— By their standards, perhaps.

— That's a pretty bleak view to have, Alan says.

— Their standards weren't bleak, Simon says. But I agree one shouldn't go down that road. Do you want to come in and have some coffee?

— I'd better not, Alan says. I've got to get to the library and then pop in and see my mother.

— How is she?

— Ageing.

— Aren't we all?

— At her age it means something.

— Give her my regards, Simon says.

— Of course. She always asks after you.

— I'm very fond of her, Simon says.

— I'll head for the bus, Alan says.

— All right. Thanks for the visit.

— Thank you for showing me the work.

— See you then.

— Yes. See you.

— How are things? Alan asks his mother as they sit in her kitchen, drinking tea.

— They could be worse.

— You're looking well.

— I could be worse. Now tell me about your book.

— You're sure you want to hear about it?

— Of course I do. I love hearing about your work.

— I haven't had much time to get on with it. Now the boys are back at school and I've got this leave I'm hoping to break the back of it.

— Why break the back?

— I mean get in so far there won't be any going back.

— I wish you'd use language precisely, she says. After all, you're a teacher of literature, so if you don't speak correctly, who will?

— I don't see that there's anything wrong with saying I'm hoping to break the back of it. Master it. That sort of thing.

— If you master a horse you break it in, she says. You don't break its back. Now tell me about the book. I like hearing about it.

— I looked again at that Rabelais passage I told you about,

he says. About the frozen —

— Hold on, his mother says. I've got to find my cigarettes.

When she is settled again he says: — That Rabelais passage about the frozen words. Remember?

She lets the smoke trickle out through her nostrils and, as it has always seemed to him since he first noticed it as a five-year-old, her ears.

— Pantagruel and Panurge and their companions reach an island, he says, and start to hear strange sounds of battle, guns going off, the cries of wounded men, the shouts of soldiers urging each other on, the neighing of frightened horses. That sort of thing. But there's no one about. The island seems to be deserted. They don't know what on earth's going on. Is this an enchanted island? Are they going crazy? Then their guide explains it all to them: A battle once took place in this very spot, in the middle of winter. It was very cold. In fact, it was freezing. The sounds of battle rose into the air and froze there. They've remained frozen to this day, but now it's suddenly getting warmer and they're starting to thaw. As a result the sounds that were frozen are once more being released into the air. Pantagruel and his men wander about the island and find a number of words and sounds, still in their frozen state, lying on the ground like large hailstones. They pick some of these up and as they start to melt in their hands the sounds of that ancient battle are released.

— How very weird, his mother says.

She stubs her cigarette out in the ashtray and lights another.
— It's quite funny, she says, but I don't see why it interests you so much.

— I don't know, he says. I feel there's something important being said here. This idea of words being frozen and then thawing as it gets warmer. You see, the strangeness of this new print culture of which he was now a part never ceased to fascinate Rabelais. Perhaps he's thinking here of words on the page, frozen in print, which need the warmth of a living, breathing reader to release them back into themselves.

— The printed book as sleeping princess, his mother says. What a nice idea.

— I hadn't thought of that, he says. But it's good, Mum. Perhaps I could use it as the title of my book.

— *The Sleeping Princess*?

— Why not? This business of ice and things being kept alive by it, or at least perfectly preserved, like those corpses they discover in the Alps thousands of years later, and all these people in America wanting to freeze their bodies so that when the secret of eternal life is found in a hundred years' time they can be warmed up and can partake of it, it's eerie, but it touches something very profound, doesn't it?

— Perhaps without the article, his mother says.

— How do you mean?

— Just *Sleeping Princess*.

— You're right, he says. You have such a good ear. But I think I'm on to something, don't you? The act of writing, the act of the poet or scribe, was a human act, but printing with moveable type, each letter locked in separately and then the whole page multiplied a thousandfold, then the pages folded and stitched together and the covers bound in and there it is, an object in a roomful of objects, no trace of the human hand or breath in it, and it's only when someone opens it and begins to read that it thaws and the words come alive. Then it's closed again and once more it's just an object in a roomful of objects. Rabelais loved what the new print culture could bring, he says, but he was also aware, as no one else seems to have been at the time, of the cost, of what was getting lost as well as what was being gained. And he made that one of the main themes of his book.

— I don't understand, his mother says.

— So you want me to explain it again?

— No no, she says. I'm getting tired. I'll try and think about it and you can bring me the text next time you come.

— My text or Rabelais?

— Yours. You know I always like to read what you write.

On his way home he stops at the pub. The redhead is there in her usual place by the window. He takes his drink over.

— Your friends not here tonight? he asks her.

— They haven't arrived yet, she says.

— You've been waiting long?

— Oh, I'm not waiting, she says. Why don't you sit down?

— May I?

— Well I asked you, didn't I? she says.

He sits, glancing at his watch.

— You're meeting someone? she asks.

— No, but I've got to keep an eye on the time.

— Why?

— Oh, I've got things to do.

— What sort of things?

— Various things.

— Family things?

— That too, he says.

— There's always that too, she says, laughing.

— And you?

— I'm free, she says. I'm single.

— You don't have a boyfriend?

— Oh yes, she says. But that doesn't mean I'm not free and single, does it?

— So there isn't that too, he says.

— Not with me, she says. But with men there always is.

— Let me get you a drink, he says.

— All right, she says. White wine. Ask for the dry.

When he brings it back to the table her friends have arrived. He puts it down. — I have to go, he says.

— Sit down, she says. Join us.

— Another time, he says.

Her friends have stopped talking and are looking at him. — I'll see you, he says.

— Yeah, she says.

When he gets home Sarah says: — A woman rang up.

— What woman?

— She said her name was Claude Grey. She said you were old friends from Princeton days. She said she'd met you again at Sam Susskind's. She kept calling you Alain.

— Yes, Alan says.

— She kept calling me Sarah.

— She's half French. She's been living in America for along time. She's married to that economist, Byron Grey.

— You didn't tell me you'd met her again at the Susskinds.

— Didn't I?

— Why did she keep calling you Alain?

— That's what I was called when she knew me. At Princeton.

— Do you want anything to eat?

— I'll find something in a minute, he says.

— She wants you to phone her, Sarah says.

— What about?

— She wants us to go there to dinner.

— Do you want to go?

— Why not?

— You don't like dinner parties.

— I don't mind, she says.

— OK.

— Don't forget. She left her number. It's by the phone.

— OK.

— Don't forget. I don't want her to think I didn't pass on the message.

— I'm going to be pretty busy for the next few weeks, he says. I don't know that I can go out to dinner.

— I don't care one way or the other, Sarah says. Just phone her. That's all I'm asking.

III

— Alain?

— Yes.

— It's me. Claude.

— I know.

— I left a message, Alain. I asked you to call me back.

— I know. Sarah passed it on. I've been very busy, Claude.

— You've been avoiding me.

— Not at all.

— You hoped I didn't really exist, didn't you, Alain? she says. You hoped you'd only imagined me.

— Not at all.

— It doesn't matter, she says. I told you it didn't matter. Once I had you at the end of my line.

He is silent.

Finally she says: — Alain?

— Alan.

— Alain to me, she says.

He is silent.

— It doesn't matter, she says. I told you it didn't matter.

— What doesn't matter? he says. What are you talking about?

She starts to laugh.

— Claude, he says. I'm very busy. What did you ring up about?

— I told Sarah I wanted you both to come round for a meal one evening, she says.

— Yes, he says. She passed on the message. I was going to call you.

— Alain, she says, I'd like to see you on your own sometime. Could we meet for coffee one of these days?

— I'm very tied up at the moment, Claude. I've got a book to finish and —

— Sam told me you weren't teaching this term.

— Not this term, no. That's why I have to get stuck into this book. It's worse than teaching, really, because you —

— You have time for a cup of coffee, she says. Everybody has time for that.

— Not in the next few days, he says.

— Come on, Alain, she says. I'm not going to eat you.

— I know you're not going to eat me, Claude, he says. But I happen to have to finish this book.

— Give me a date, she says.

— A date?

— Give me a time and a place where we can meet. Next week. The week after. It doesn't matter. I'm here for a while.

— Look, Claude, he says, can I give you a call when I've —

— I'd rather we fixed it now, she says.

— But I'm just not quite sure, Claude. Not quite sure how things are going to pan out. You must know how it is.

— You're trying to avoid me, Alain, she says.

— Not at all, he says.

— It doesn't matter, she says.

He is silent.

— How about Monday week? she says. Eleven o'clock.

He is silent. Then he says: — Where?

— You say.

— What about the Orangery in Holland Park?

— Is that easy to find?

— It's in the middle of the Park. You can't miss it. They do good coffee.

— I'm writing it down, she says.

He is silent.

— How are you, Alain? she asks.

— Alan.

— Alain to me, she says.

— As you wish, he says.

— How are you?

— Fine, he says. Fine.

— I'm fine too, she says. That makes two of us.

He is silent.

— What are you writing, Alain? she asks.

— Perhaps we could leave that till we meet? he says.

— Of course, she says. I was just curious.

— Claude, he says, are you sure you want us to meet?

— Of course, she says. That's what I've come here for.

— Don't be silly.

— I have. Honest.

He is silent. Then he says: — I don't know what you mean.

— It doesn't matter, she says. She begins to laugh.

— I have to go, Claude, he says.

— No you don't, she says. That's always your first reaction: I have to go. Why can't you talk to me?

— I am talking to you.

— Properly, she says.

— I don't like talking on the phone, he says. I don't like not seeing the person I'm talking to.

— I know what you mean, she says. That's why we should meet soon.

He is silent.

— I'm really enjoying my time here, she says.

— Oh yes? he says.

— Yes, she says. Very much. I'm so glad I came.

— And Byron?

— He always enjoys himself. As long as he's working. He was sorry to miss you the other day.

He is silent.

— The only worry is Sophie, she says.

— She still hasn't settled down?

— She's a sensitive child, she says. She misses her friends.

— I see.

— Do you think she'd get on with your boys?

— I don't think so, he says. They prefer football to girls at the moment.

— She could learn to play.

— Claude, he says. I really have to go now.

— Of course, she says. I'm sorry to have taken up your time.

— You haven't.

— You didn't mind my ringing?

— No, I'm pleased.

— So am I, she says. I'll see you in the Orangery in Holland Park on Monday week. Eleven o'clock. Don't forget.

He is silent.

— Alain? she says.

— Yes?

— Are you still there?

He is silent.

— It doesn't matter, she says. Even if you forget. I'll just keep on trying. You know that, don't you?

— I won't forget, he says.

— Goodbye, Alain.

— Goodbye, he says.

IV

She is already there when he arrives, sitting at a table in the corner.

— I'm late, he says. I'm sorry.

She smiles up at him.

He takes off his coat and slings it on a chair. He sits down opposite her. — Have you been waiting long? he asks.

— All day, she says.

— I thought we said eleven o'clock?

— Of course we did. I've only just got here.

They sit.

— Well well, she says at last.

— Well well what?

She smiles at him.

— What do you mean? he says.

She shrugs her shoulders, laughs.

— You mean... that we're here?

— Yes, she says. And other things.

— What other things?

The waiter stands at their table.

— Coffee? Alan asks her.

— Yes please.

— They do nice cakes here.

— Yes please.

— Good.

— Coffee for two and the tray of cakes, Alan says.

The waiter goes.

— I'm a great eater, you know, she says.

— I remember, he says. But it doesn't show.

— Thank you, she says. You were always so polite.

— It's the truth, he says.

— I think, she says, it's because there's a wolf inside me who chews it all up and digests it.

— A wolf?

— Uhuh.

— What do you mean, a wolf?

The waiter returns with the coffee and a tray of cakes.

— Oh good, she says. Éclairs. And millefeuilles. My favourites.

— What do you mean, a wolf? he repeats when the waiter has gone.

— It means I'm always hungry and I never seem to grow fat. She laughs and puts a hand on his arm. — You should see your face, Alain, she says.

He pours the coffee.

She takes an éclair from the tray and begins to eat.

— Yes please, he says.

— What?

— Yes please.

— I don't understand.

— You haven't lost your French mannerisms, he says.

— What do you mean?

— Don't you remember?

— What? she says, finishing the cake and wiping her mouth with her napkin.

— The English say please and the French say yes please. Because please in French means no thank you. Don't you remember? I used to try to correct you.

— I don't remember, she says.

He sips his coffee.

She leans back in her chair. — I read all your books, Alain, she says.

— Alan.

She waves a hand, acknowledging the correction.

— I wonder why, he says.

— I'm interested.

— In me or the subject-matter?

— Both, she says.

— They're not exactly page-turners, he says.

— I like the tone, she says.

He sips his coffee.

— Alain, she says.

— Alan.

— When I knew you you were Alain Schnaidaire.

He is silent, looking at her.

— That, I seem to recall, is what brought us together, she says. You must meet him, my friends said. Your French mother. His Swiss father. Alain Schnaidaire.

— How is your mother?

— Dead.

— I'm sorry.

She shrugs. — As you know, we never got on. Do you want

to know how she died?

— If you like.

— No, she says. It's of no interest.

— And your father?

— He's on to his third wife.

— Third?

— Yes.

— What happened to the second?

— She threw him out for sleeping with his students. He would bring them home after his seminars and hump them on the living-room couch. In the end she got fed up and had the locks changed so that when he got home he couldn't get in. So he married the one he was with at the time and took early retirement and is now living in Greece.

— Is that nice for you?

— For me?

— I mean being able to visit him in Greece.

— I don't, she says. His wife doesn't like me.

— I see.

— She's my age. Younger.

— She could be your age and still like you.

— Yes, but she doesn't.

— And your father doesn't want to see his granddaughter?

— No. He was never very strong on family feelings.

— I see.

— You know, she says, I think I'm going to have another.

She puts a millefeuille on her plate. — I sometimes think the wolf won't let me alone till my mission is accomplished, she says.

— What mission?

She shrugs.

— Your work? he asks.

— Don't be silly, she says.

— Why silly?

— Have you read my books?

— Well...

— Be honest.

— I read the first one, he says.

— *The Song of the Wind?*

— I think so.

— You don't know?

— I think that's what it was called.

— About Siberia.

— That's the one.

She eats.

— Don't tell me, she says.

— Tell you what?

— What you thought of it.

— I'm no judge, he says.

— Yes you are, she says, putting down her fork. That's exactly what you are.

He is silent.

— So? she says.

— I didn't get on with it.

— That's what I mean.

— What?

— They're not for the discerning reader. They're just something I do.

— Why?

— I don't know. It's the only thing I know how to do, perhaps. And it's fun, sometimes.

— The money must be handy.

— We don't need it. Not with Byron's salary.

— Do you want to do something better? he asks.

— If I could, she says, yes. But then I'd like to fly.

— You could try.

— Flying?

— Writing what you would consider better.

— That's tough, she says.

He shrugs.

— Tell me about yourself, she says.

— There's nothing to tell.

— Yes there is. There always is. What kind of a life do you lead? Are you happy?

— All that.

— Ah, he says. All that.

— What about your children?

— What about them?

— Do you get on with them?

— I think so, he says. You'd have to ask them.

— Oh, Alain, she says. Only you would ever say a thing like that.

— Really?

— Yes. Really.

She laughs and leans across the table, putting a hand on his arm. — You look so frightened, she says.

— Me?

— I won't eat you, you know.

— I know.

— You know? How do you know? Perhaps I've come here to do precisely that.

— Have you?

— You never know, do you? She laughs. Go on, she says.

42

What happened with Anna?

— We divorced.

— So Sam told me. I liked Anna.

— Why do you ask if you know?

— I thought you might tell me a bit more than the bare facts.

— No, he says. That's all there is to tell.

— And Sarah?

— What about her? Where did you meet?

— At the fishmonger's.

— You're teasing me, Alain.

He smiles.

— Oh well, she says. I'll have to ask her.

— I wouldn't, he says.

— Why?

— She might think you were being nosy.

— I'm sure I could do it discreetly.

He shrugs.

— Tell me about what you're writing then, she says.

— It wouldn't interest you.

— Why do you say that? she says. I told you. I read all your books. I always liked what you wrote.

She looks at the plate of cakes. — Do you think I should have another? she asks him.

— Why not? If you feel like it.

— I'll try the chocolate slice, she says.

She helps herself. He pours her another cup of coffee.

— Go on, she says. Tell me.

— It's a book about the coming of print, he says. Plenty's been written about it, but mainly by historians. We've had books about Protestantism and print, books about print and the rise of the bourgeoisie, books about print and the city, and of course books about print and education. But no one has really explored the effect of print on writers. I mean from the inside. How it was transforming their sense of what they were doing and could do. Ong and McLuhan touched on it, but too often in their hands it turned into a version of the Fall. I want to be more neutral. And more specific. I want to look in detail at three writers, Rabelais, Cervantes and Sterne, who all benefited greatly from the new print culture but who all understood instinctively that there was also something devilish about print – that it allowed you to do just what you wanted, owing allegiance to no one except the market. So long as enough people bought your book for it to pay its way you were free to say exactly what you liked. But at the same time print robbed you of any authority and made anything you said automatically meaningless.

– Why meaningless?

– Because a gap had opened up between the person who wrote and the person who read. Dante and Chaucer could see themselves as educators and entertainers, someone commissioned their work and people gathered to hear them read. But these new writers of the print culture were invisible and beholden to no one but themselves – and the market. That gave them a lot of freedom but at the same time it robbed them of any authority.

– That sounds like another version of the Fall too, she says.

– Maybe. But it was a personal Fall.

– Isn't the Fall always personal?

– Not for Catholics it isn't.

– Well, she says, a Protestant version then.

– You're right, he says. Protestantism was just one take on a distinctive late medieval crisis. But I want to keep away from general topics and focus on my three authors – I'm not boring you?

– Boring me? she says. No.

– I go on so.

– You always did, she says. I liked that.

– Well, he says, you always seemed to understand what I was talking about, even when I didn't understand it myself. Much more than my learned colleagues.

She pushes the plate away from her, touches her mouth with her napkin. – *Basta!* she says. If I eat any more I'll burst.

They sit in silence.

Finally she says: – Did you ever think we'd meet again, Alain?

– Why not? he says. These days...

– Ah, she says. These days. So easy to escape. So easy to pursue.

She takes her diary out of her bag. – We have to fix up this dinner, she says. Byron is very keen to see you. And I'd like to meet Sarah.

– The thing is, he says, she's not very good with dinner parties.

– What do you mean, not very good?

– She finds it difficult being with a lot of people.

– Difficult?

– Uhuh.

– Well, she says, there needn't be a lot of people. If you like it can just be the four of us.

– No no, he says. You do what you normally do. I'll see if I can persuade her. But I can't promise anything.

– We were thinking of Friday week. The seventh.

– I'll talk to her.

— You don't want to pencil it in?

— No. I'll talk to her first. Then ring you. But don't hold
up the arrangements because of us.

— But it's you we want.

— I'll ring you.

— You won't, of course, she says.

— Yes I will, he says.

They sit.

— Alain, she says. I have to go.

— Already?

— I have to take Sophie to the dentist.

She picks up the bill and stands up.

— No, he says, putting his hand over hers.

— Please, she says. It was my idea.

— You think you made a mistake? he asks.

— Mistake? she says.

— That your idea was a mistake.

— My id – ? She laughs. Why do you say that?

— You suddenly seemed to lose interest.

— I have a daughter to get to the dentist.

— All right, he says. But I pay this time.

She is waiting for him at the entrance.

Together they stand and look at the rain.

— Good old England, she says. Everything they say about it
is true.

— You think so?

— Well, isn't it?

— In a way that's not true of France or Italy? Or America?

— Yes, she says. One day in those countries shows you it's
not the set of clichés you were carrying around in your head.
But a month in England only convinces you that all the clichés

were accurate representations of reality.

— It's not that bad, he says.

— Oh, she says, many of the clichés are good. But they're still clichés.

She takes her umbrella out of her bag and opens it.

They stand.

— Is that it then? he asks.

— Is what it?

— I don't know. It's so abrupt.

— What is?

— Your getting up like that. After wanting to see me so much.

— You never listen, do you? she says. I told you I had to get a daughter to the dentist.

They stand.

— You're right, she says. Don't you remember? I was always like that. You were hard to get hold of and I was hard to hold still.

She takes his hand. — It's a start, isn't it? she says. After all those years.

He is silent.

— I needed to hear your voice, she says. To sit and look at you.

— I see, he says.

She lets go his hand. — Anyway, she says, we'll have lots more chances to talk. Now I'm in London. Won't we?

— I don't know, he says. I'm going to be very busy with my book.

She starts to laugh and after a while, reluctantly, he joins in.

— There's Friday week to begin with, she says.

— I'll talk to Sarah, he says. I can't promise anything.

— We'll expect you both, she says. Eight o'clock.

She steps out into the rain, opening her umbrella.

— I'll walk with you, he says.

— No, she says.

— Why not?

— I'd rather not, she says.

She pecks his cheek. — *Au revoir*, Alain, she says.

He watches her walk away, her head hidden by the umbrella.

V

— There was really no need for you to come, Ronnie Chinn says.

— I wanted to, Alan says.

Ronnie Chinn stands in the open doorway. He passes a hand over his face.

— How are you? Alan asks.

— You'd better come in, Ronnie Chinn says.

They stand in the hall.

— Traffic was terrible, Alan says.

— It always is, Ronnie Chinn says. He shuts the door and locks it. — Would you like some coffee? he asks.

— That would be nice, Alan says.

— The cleaning lady was supposed to come, Ronnie Chinn says. But her mother is ill.

— They always are, Alan says.

— Are what? Ronnie Chinn asks.

— Ill.

— Oh yes, Ronnie Chinn says.

They stand.

— Did I ask you if you wanted some coffee? Ronnie Chinn asks.

— Yes, Alan says. I said yes.

Ronnie Chinn wanders off towards the kitchen.

— Do you want me in the kitchen? Alan asks.

— What? Ronnie Chinn says.

— Shall I come in with you while you make the coffee?

— Oh yes, Ronnie Chinn says. Please.

They stand in the kitchen.

Alan sits at the kitchen table. Ronnie Chinn stands looking out of the window.

— How are things? Alan asks.

— What?

— I wondered how you were coping.

— Terrible, Ronnie Chinn says. I feel terrible all the time.

Alan is silent.

— I've felt terrible ever since Jane left me, Ronnie Chinn says.

Ronnie Chinn fills the kettle and plugs it in.

— Doesn't the work help? Alan asks.

— I feel terrible at work, Ronnie Chinn says.

He stares down at the kettle, which is beginning to make a noise. — And then with my father dying, he says.

— He had a good life, Alan says.

The kettle comes to the boil and then switches itself off.

— Nothing prepares you for these things, he says.

Alan sits in silence.

— He had a miserable life, Ronnie Chinn says. Ever since my mother died.

He takes a tin of Nescafé out of the cupboard and stands, holding it in his hand.

Alan waits.

– He couldn't get over Jane leaving me, he says.

He takes two mugs off the shelf and sets them down on the table.

Alan waits. Finally he says: – Make it a flat spoonful for me.

– You see, Ronnie Chinn says, I felt as if I'd let him down.

– Aren't you imagining things? Alan asks.

– Imagining things? Ronnie Chinn says.

– It wasn't your fault, Alan says. These things happen.

– I don't know. Ronnie Chinn says. How do you want your coffee? he asks.

– One flat spoonful, Alan says. Milk and sugar.

– I have some sugar somewhere, Ronnie Chinn says.

He rummages in the cupboard. – Here it is, he says.

He puts the packet on the table.

– I'm going to need a spoon, Alan says.

– Of course, Ronnie Chinn says.

He finds a spoon and hands it to him, then sits down opposite him.

Alan digs into the packet, puts the sugar in his coffee, stirs, puts the spoon back on the table and sips his coffee.

– He couldn't understand it, he says. Neither could I.

– You're in touch? Alan asks.

– No, Ronnie Chinn says. Not a word from her.

Alan sits, sipping his coffee.

– It never seemed to happen in his generation, Ronnie Chinn says.

– Yes it did, Alan says.

Ronnie Chinn is looking out of the window.

Finally Alan says: – Drink up. Your coffee'll get cold.

— He took it personally, Ronnie Chinn says.

— You don't think you're projecting? Alan asks.

Ronnie Chinn pushes his mug away from him, then pulls it back towards him.

— You were in love with her? Alan asks.

Ronnie Chinn stares at him.

— These things happen, Alan says.

— I thought they happened to other people, Ronnie Chinn says.

— One always does, Alan says.

— It's terrible to feel I contributed to his death, Ronnie Chinn says.

— How could you contribute to his death? Alan says. You weren't responsible for the breakup.

— I didn't give him any grandchildren, Ronnie Chinn says. I didn't give my mother any grandchildren.

— You didn't want children?

— I don't know, Ronnie Chinn says. It just didn't happen.

— Isn't it better that way? Alan asks. Think how you'd be feeling now if she'd taken your children with her.

— They'd still be there.

Alan empties his mug and puts it down on the table.

— I feel I failed them, he says.

— That's a ridiculous thing to say, Alan says. It's got nothing to do with them.

— Other people all seem to have children, Ronnie Chinn says.

— Not everyone, Alan says.

— Nearly everyone, Ronnie Chinn says. They do nothing but talk about them.

— You've got plenty of time, Alan says. That's the advantage of being a man.

— But my parents are dead, Ronnie Chinn says.

— It's got nothing to do with them, Alan says.

— You don't understand, Ronnie Chinn says.

— No, Alan says. I don't.

Ronnie Chinn plays with his cup, staring out of the window.

— I'm sorry, Alan says.

— I told you I wasn't much fun to be with, Ronnie Chinn says.

— I didn't come here to have fun, Alan says. I came to see you.

— It was very good of you, Ronnie Chinn says. You must be very busy.

— That's all right, Alan says. I wanted to come.

They sit in silence.

— I think I ought to go now though, Alan says.

— It was good of you to come, Ronnie Chinn says.

They stand at the door.

— You seem to have even less time when you're on leave, Alan says. What with one thing and another.

Ronnie Chinn does not move.

— It was good to see you, Alan says. Take care.

— Goodbye, Ronnie Chinn says, closing the door carefully.

Alan walks down the road in the autumn drizzle.

VI

— It's not really the kind of thing that can easily be explained, Byron says. To the non-specialist.

The girl with the red hair laughs. — I don't understand anything about anything anyway, she says, so why not try it out on me and see?

— I think it might be better not, Byron says.

— You make it sound like pornography or something, the girl says.

— Oh, pornography's much more interesting, Byron says.

— Why? the girl asks.

— Why? Byron says. He cups his chin in his hand. Well, he says, there are various reasons.

— Give me some of them, the girl says.

He is silent, stroking his chin.

— Go on, the girl says. You must be able to think of a few.

— I don't think we'd better go down that road, Byron says.

The girl laughs, showing her gums.

— You think they've beaten racism on the terraces? Sam

Susskind says. You should have been at Stamford Bridge on Saturday.

— Alan wanted to take the boys, Sarah says, but then Adam came down with flu.

— I tell you, Sam Susskind says, I had to wrap my nose in my handkerchief.

— Because of the smell?

— Smell? Sam Susskind says. You've got to be joking. Because I didn't want them to see I was Jewish.

— Oh come on, Sarah says.

— Honest, Sam Susskind says. These guys frighten me to death. One minute they're screaming abuse at some poor black sod trying to make a living kicking a ball and the next minute they could be turning on you and sticking a knife into your stomach just because you're Jewish.

— First of all you're exaggerating, Sarah says, and then I don't see how they can know you're Jewish.

— How they can know? Sam Susskind says, staring at her, his eyes open wide. How they can know? Sarah, baby, he says, you're the only person in the whole effing world who can't see I look like everyone's worse nightmare of a Jew.

— You're paranoid, Sarah says.

— Of course I'm paranoid, he says. I'm Jewish, aren't I?

— Not Jewish, Sarah says. American Jewish. We don't feel like that here.

— You know why, don't you? Sam Susskind says.

— Tell me.

— Because you're all dead, Sam Susskind says. D-e-a-d. Dead.

— How do you figure that out? Sarah says.

— Because if you're a Jew and you're alive you have to be paranoid.

— You talk a lot of balls, don't you, Sam? Sarah says.

They are talking football at the other end of the table as well.

— They'd only go to bed, Alan says, if I promised to watch the second half and write a full report and leave it by their beds for them to read first thing in the morning.

— You had to sit and watch the whole second half? Claude says.

— Oh, I would have, anyway, Alan says. It was just that when it was over I didn't feel like writing a report on it. That took me another fifteen minutes.

— I'm surprised it only took you that long, she says.

— I wasn't filing it for the *Times*, Alan says. But it's amazing how even with your own children you don't want to sound inelegant.

— All I can say is I'm glad Sophie has no interest in sport whatsoever, Claude says.

— What's she interested in then?

— Clothes, Claude says. And boys.

— Boys? At her age?

— I was interested in boys at her age, Claude says.

— Well, you, Alan says.

— Weren't you interested in girls at that age?

— I can't remember.

— Of course you can, she says.

He can feel the warmth of her leg against his. — Perhaps I was, he says. But then I was ashamed of it.

— Alain, she says. You know what I'd really like?

— What?

— I'd like to see the sea with you. To walk along a beach.

— The sea? he says.

— Will you take me one of these days?

— Of course, he says

— Thank you, Alain, she says.

— Don't thank me, he says. I haven't done it yet.

— But you will, won't you? she says. Now you've promised?

— The way the Treasury works, Byron says to the white-haired lady on his other side, is so arcane you probably not only have to be English to understand it, you have to have two English grandmothers. I don't think I'll ever be able to master the mixture of silence and innuendo that appears to be the norm here.

— Then why did they ask you? the white-haired lady asks.

— It makes them feel good to have an American in their midst, Byron says. That's what I'm here for. It's called the feel-good factor in economics.

— That's weird, the white-haired lady says.

— Economics is weird, Byron says. Government is weird. Put the two together and you have something seriously weird.

— I was so drunk, the red-haired girl's partner says to Jeanie Susskind, that I followed him in. I didn't realise it was that sort of place.

Jeanie Susskind laughs.

— This is delicious, Alan says. He can still feel the warmth of her leg against his.

— Don't change the subject, Claude says.

— I wanted to say it before it was too late.

— Too late?

— Before we'd moved on to the next course. It would look odd if I suddenly said: — This is very good and so was the previous dish.

She rings a little bell by her plate. — Paola, she says to the sleepy-eyed girl who is helping out, will you make sure everyone has had enough and then move on to the next course?

— Yes, Mrs Grey, the girl says. She leans over the white-haired lady: — You want more? she asks.

— Oh, God, Claude says. Won't they ever send me someone with style?

Sam Susskind says to Sarah: — I'll show you if you want. He puts his hand in his mouth and takes out his dentures. You see? he says, pointing to a molar.

— I can't believe this, Jeanie Susskind says, gazing across the table at him. I just can't believe it.

— It was quite dark, the red-haired girl's partner says, especially coming off the glare of the street. But then I began to make out shapes and —

— I knew he'd do something like that, Jeanie Susskind says. I knew it from the moment he said he wanted his polka-dotted bow tie.

Sam Susskind puts his teeth back into his mouth. Sarah laughs again.

— Parrots, the red-haired girl's partner says. It was full of parrots. I couldn't believe it. I thought they must be stuffed or something, it was dark in there, it was difficult to see, but then my eyes began to adjust and blow me if they weren't all real.

— If we didn't forget we wouldn't be able to function at all, Alan says. Like that character in Borges.

— So why do some people remember more than others? Claude says.

— You remember as much as you need, he says.

— But how does one define need? she asks.

— That's a good question, he says.

— I was always good at the questions, she says.

Paola serves the dessert.

— It's good to see you again, Alan, Byron says as they sit in the living-room with their coffee.

— And you, Byron, Alan says. How are you liking it over here?

— I love it here, Byron says. I really love it over here in England.

— So why didn't you come here before?

— Oh, I come over quite a lot, Byron says. But only for short stays. Fly in fly out, you know what it's like, take in a show or two, see a few people you have to see and that's it.

Alan sips his coffee.

— Mind you, Byron says, I complain that I'm not allowed to get on with my work in Harvard in peace, but I quite like the buzz of dealing with politicians, big issues, you know?

— Uhuh, Alan says.

— There's nothing quite like it, you know? Byron says.

— They keep you busy, do they?

— Well, it's different this time, Byron says. It's a long-term thing. There's a chance to settle in and do things my way. You know what I mean? And to have the family here, it makes a whole load of difference.

— I'm only a dancer, the red-haired girl says to Sarah. I just do what I'm told.

— I'm sure you don't, Sarah says.

— You have to, the red-haired girl says. That's the first thing you learn in ballet school. If you don't and they know you don't you may never get work again. Shut your mouth and do what you're told. In the end, she says, you're only a cog in a giant wheel.

— I wish I was even that, Sarah says.

— It's not much fun being a cog, the red-haired girl says. I can tell you.

— But to be a part of something, Sarah says.

— But what if you don't like the thing you're part of? the girl says. For every piece you do that you believe in there are a dozen you think are rubbish. Or you think the choreographer's rubbish. Or your partner's rubbish. Know what I mean?

— I hadn't thought of it like that, Sarah says.

— We play every Sunday morning, Sam says to the red-haired girl's partner, whose name turns out to be Zaph, ph, not f. Eleven o'clock.

— Last time I played I didn't warm up properly and did my knee in, Zaph says. I don't want to repeat the experience.

— That was stupid, Sam Susskind says. Really stupid.

— I thought I was still nineteen, Zaph says. It took me six months to recover. I had to go to physiotherapy twice a week. And the knee still hurts when it's cold.

— What sort of a pitch was it? Sam Susskind asks.

— One of those indoor inflatable things, Zaph says. I tried to turn with the first ball that came to me and something went in my knee. I almost screamed with pain.

— It's different out of doors, Sam Susskind says. These indoor arenas with artificial floors are hell.

— I'm not sure I want to risk it, Zaph says.

— Everyone has a good time, Sam Susskind says. We play hard but we also eat and drink pretty hard afterwards.

— I'll think about it, Zaph says.

— We need a keeper, Sam Suskind says. You're just what we need.

— I can't stand it when he takes his teeth out like that in

front of everybody, Jeanie Susskind says.

— Nobody pays any attention, Claude says.

— I feel it's so coarse, Jeanie Susskind says. Do you know what I mean?

— Come and have tea next week, Claude says.

— I suppose I knew the kind of man he was when I married him, Jeanie Susskind says. But somehow it doesn't get any easier with time.

— He's his own person, Claude says. How many people can you say that of?

— I hate myself when I feel like that, Jeanie Susskind says. It makes me feel such a snob.

— Everyone's a snob somewhere or other, Claude says.

— If you've grown up in a certain way, Jeanie Susskind says, with certain values, it's not easy to change, is it?

Alan looks round the room and sneaks a glance at his watch.

— You found a nice house, he says.

— The Chancellor was here the other night, Byron says. He says they looked for a house in this street.

— Really? Alan says.

— He says they really liked it. They liked the trees.

— We monitor the Arab world, the white-haired lady says to Sam Susskind. We monitor school textbooks in particular. After all, if we're subsidising some of those countries to the extent that we are we should have a say in what they teach at school don't you think? Some of that stuff is beyond belief.

— It won't make any difference, Sam Susskind says to the white-haired lady. So long as they preach what they do in the mosques.

— I don't think you're right there, the white-haired lady says. Our research shows that if you can get textbooks in the schools to tell the truth it makes a huge difference. It sows the seeds of freedom of thought.

— I think we should be going, Alan says, getting up. Sarah's only just got over the flu.

— It was great to see you, Byron says, rising with him.

— And you, Alan says.

Claude comes towards them.

— We ought to be going, Alan says.

— So early?

— Sarah's only just got over the flu.

— I'm going to like her, Claude says. I can tell.

Sarah is at his side. — Thank you so much, she says. It was a lovely meal.

— My pleasure, Claude says. Take care.

VII

Leaving the bathing-ponds behind him, he strikes out in the direction of Kenwood. Halfway up the hill he hears someone calling his name. He turns and waits for the caller to catch up with him.

— Hi, she says.

— Hullo to you.

— Do you remember me?

— People are always asking me that, he says. Do I look the forgetful type?

— I just wondered, she says.

— How could I forget you? he says. You're the lady who enjoys doing nothing.

— And you're the man with the footballing sons.

They walk on up the hill.

— Sam tells me you're a brilliant scholar, she says.

— You mustn't pay any attention to what Sam says.

— Modest too? she says.

— Look, he says, all Sam's friends are brilliant. At his house you're sure to meet the most brilliant TV producer in Malawi and the most brilliant surfer in County Cork, not to speak of the most brilliant proofreader in Antigua.

— I wish someone would say that about me, she says.

— But they do, he says. They say you have the most beautiful smile in the whole of England.

— They do?

— Absolutely.

— You're pulling my leg.

— Why would I do a thing like that?

— To satisfy your latent sadism.

— Ask Sam, he says.

— Can one ask a thing like that, do you think?

— Why not?

— A beautiful smile's not the same thing as producing, is it? Or surfing, or what was it? Proofreading?

— No, he says. No.

— I mean you haven't earned it, have you?

— I don't know, he says. A beautiful smile's not exactly a beautiful nose, is it?

— What a peculiar conversation we're having, she says.

— It's your influence, he says. The last time, if my memory isn't at fault, it was ski-ing down Everest.

They walk.

— I didn't think you lived in this part of the world, she says.

— I don't. I'm going to see a rabbi.

— You're religious?

— I'm not religious and I'm not a Jew. He's a friend.

— I'd like to know a rabbi, she says.

— You can. Come with me.

— No. I have to see my mother-in-law.

— How dutiful.

— I like her.

— Can't she wait?

— No. She's expecting me.

— Pity, he says.

— Another time, perhaps.

— He'd love to meet you. He's partial to beautiful women.

— Hey! she says. First it was the smile and now it's —

— But it's true, he says. He's a devout family man who's always surrounded by beautiful and intelligent women. I don't know how he does it.

— Can we get off that subject, please?

— As you like, he says.

They walk.

— I like these chance encounters, she says. They make me feel there's a Providence looking down on the world.

They walk.

— Chaucer has a tale, he says, in which the most improbable meetings and coincidences occur. The narrator always prefaces these with the phrase, 'Whether by aventure or cas', that is, whether by chance or providence, leaving it delightfully open for you to decide which it is.

— I've never read Chaucer, she says. Not since school.

— You should, he says. He has a lot to say to us today.

— Is that why one reads? she asks.

He laughs. — I'm sorry, he says.

— Why sorry?

— I was being both condescending and didactic. A bad habit teachers get into.

— I didn't notice, she says. I go off here, she says, stopping.

— Do you? What a shame.

She laughs.

— Do you want to give me your phone number? he says. Then we can go and see my friend one day.

— Why don't we put ourselves in the hands of chance — what was it, aventure? or Providence? she says, laughing.

— We could nudge Providence a little, couldn't we?

— It wouldn't be the same then, would it?

— No, he agrees. I suppose not.

— Goodbye, she says, holding up her face to be kissed.

He kisses her cheek. — Goodbye, Cynthia, he says.

She walks away across the Heath.

Miriam opens the door. — Hullo! she says. He's upstairs. Bathing Seth.

— Shall I go up?

— Yes. Go on. I'm in the middle.

She hurries back down the corridor. He climbs the narrow stairs.

The bathroom door is open. — Come on in, Mike calls out. We're almost finished.

He steps inside the bathroom.

— Say Hullo to Alan, Mike says to his son.

— Hullo, Alan says. He leans over and rubs the child's head. Good, is it? he asks.

Mike holds out a towel. — Come on, he says.

Alan watches him dry his son. He does it slowly and with care, passing the towel between each toe, turning the child round, rubbing his ears.

— There, he says. Go to bed and Mummy'll be along to read to you.

— I haven't washed my teeth.

66

— Brushed.

— What's the difference?

— You wash your hands and brush your teeth.

— But sometimes I brush my hands. To get the nails clean.

— Stop showing off, his father says. We haven't got all day.

— I'll wait downstairs, Alan says.

— I'll be with you in a minute.

Alan closes the door and goes down the stairs into the slightly musty smelling living-room.

In a few minutes Mike joins him. — I could do with a drink, he says. And you?

— Please.

— Scotch?

— Fine.

— Water? Ice?

— As it is.

— After twenty years you forget what it's like having a child that age, Mike says, pouring and handing him a glass.

— Cheers.

Mike sits down opposite him and lets out a long sigh.

— Don't say you don't enjoy it, Alan says.

— I didn't say that. Only that I'd forgotten how tiring it was having a three-year-old. And you? How're things?

— OK.

— Enjoying your sabbatical?

— No.

— No?

— You know how it is. When you're working you convince yourself that if only you had the time you could get on with what you really want to do. When you've finally got the time you wonder if you're up to it.

— Of course.

— If you're any good.

— Of course.

— Suddenly your whole life and *raison d'être* is in question.

— Of course.

— So it's not just me?

— You know it isn't, Mike says.

— I don't know which is worse, Alan says, being alone and different or being one of the masses.

— You're different all right, Mike says. We all are.

— Oh, God, Alan says. To live with that for the whole of one's life. I don't know that I can bear it.

— It's not easy, Mike says.

— I have this fantasy, Alan says, that when we're gone there'll just be all the words we've ever spoken, hanging there in the breeze, and that'll be us. What we were. Are. Do you know what I mean? No context, no explanation, just the words — us.

— What a thought! Mike says. He gets up. Another? he asks.

Alan holds out his glass. — It'll be up to those who see the words to breathe life into them. To reconstitute the person.

— You forget other people, Mike says. What you mean to other people.

— But that's as nebulous as what I mean to myself, Alan says. Only the words are out there, public.

— I don't think it's nebulous, Mike says. I think it's very real.

— It may be real, Alan says, but it vanishes with the people. Only the words remain. Of course they don't either, but that's my fantasy.

— You've said things you're ashamed of? Mike asks.

— Haven't we all? Alan says. But it isn't a question of shame, really.

68

Mike sips his drink and gazes at him under his thick eyebrows.

— There's a woman pursuing me, Alan says. I knew her ages ago in the States. She's over here now with her family. She says she's come to find me.

— Why?

— I don't know.

— You must have an idea. Did you have an affair?

— I don't know.

— What do you mean you don't know?

— I'm not sure.

— How can you not be sure? It's not exactly…

— It doesn't matter, Alan says.

— Why do you think she's pursuing you then?

— I don't know. I'm not even sure that she is.

— I'm afraid you've lost me there, his friend says.

— I'm not sure, Alan says, I may be imagining it.

— Why do you think she might be?

— She said so.

— She said so? And what did you say?

— Nothing.

— Nothing? You let it pass?

— She may have been joking.

— You don't know if she was joking or not?

— She was always like that.

— Like what?

— I mean I never quite knew where I stood with her. And I don't now. The only thing I know is that I'm afraid of her.

— She has something on you?

— I don't know.

— You don't know much, do you? Mike says. He finishes his drink. Another? he asks.

69

— No thanks, Alan says. I'm sorry, he says.

— Go on, Mike says. Tell me more.

— I think she thinks she does.

— Does what?

— Have something on me.

— So there was something?

— I don't know.

— You've lost me again, Mike says.

— It's too complicated to go into, Alan says. I don't know myself.

— Was that what you said you wanted to talk to me about?

— Yes.

— Then talk.

— It's too complicated. I thought talking would help but now I see it doesn't.

— How do you know? You haven't got going yet.

— I can't, Alan says.

Mike gets up and fixes himself another drink. — Are you still attracted to her? he asks from the drinks table.

— I am and I'm not, Alan says. There are moments when I am, terribly, and then others when I'm appalled by her.

— But you're not indifferent?

— It may be fear, Alan says.

— Fear of what?

— I don't know.

His friend is silent, staring at him. Then he says: — And Sarah?

— She's out of it.

— Out of it?

— She doesn't know anything.

— I see, Mike says. He sips his drink. What are you going to do? he asks.

— I don't know, Alan says.

— Forget her, Mike says.

— That's what I've done till now. But now she's come to England to do something to me and I'm frightened.

— Perhaps you're frightened by your continuing attraction to her.

— Perhaps.

— What do you intend to do? Mike asks.

— I don't know, Alan says.

— She's threatened you?

— No. Of course not.

— Why of course? How should I know?

— I'm sorry. You couldn't. But she's come over with her husband who's a big shot advising the government on economics and she engineered a meeting with me and now she's pursuing me.

— Go to the police.

— Don't be silly. It isn't like that. And anyway, I may just be imagining it.

— Well, if you've got nothing to feel ashamed or guilty about and she isn't really threatening you, you can relax.

— Yes.

— Except that you obviously can't.

— Exactly.

— Because you feel guilty?

— No. Because I don't know.

— And you won't try to explain?

— It's too complicated. I'm sorry.

— Don't worry, Mike says. I'm always there if you change your mind.

— I'm sorry, Alan says again, He gets up. It's a mess, he says.

— No, Mike says. It's life.

— Is it?

— Of course, Mike says, accompanying him to the door. Remember, he says as he opens it, I'm always there. Just pick up the phone. Any time you want to talk about it.

— Believe me, Alan says on the doorstep, I do. Only there seems to be nothing to talk about, does there?

On the way home he stops at the pub. The redhead is there by herself.

— On your own? he asks.

— As you can see, she says.

— May I join you?

— Get me another drink first.

— What is it?

— White wine. Ask for the dry.

When he sits down she says: — I haven't seen you around for a while.

— I've been busy.

— What do you do?

— I'm a teacher.

— My friend's a teacher, she says.

— Your boyfriend?

— No. My girlfriend.

She sips her drink.

— You're not going to ask me what I teach? he asks.

— Why?

— I don't know. People usually do.

— You're a funny bloke, she says.

— And you? he asks. What do you do?

— I'm not working at the moment.

— But when you are?

— Buy me another drink, will you? she says.

— Your friend's not coming?

— Nah.

When he sits down again he says to her: — Perhaps we could go for a little walk when you've finished.

— What for?

— It's a nice evening. I thought we could have a stroll.

— What for?

— I don't know. I thought it would be nice.

— Nah, she says. I don't like walking.

— Really? he says. Why?

— My ankles swell up if I walk, she says. I can't sleep then.

— You should see a doctor, he says.

— I prefer not to walk.

— It was just a thought, he says.

— You're a funny bloke, she says.

He glances at his watch.

— You've got to go, she says.

— Well...

— When men look at their watches they're trying to get away, she says.

— Really? he says. Not women?

— Nah.

— Why do you think that is?

— What do you mean?

— Why do you think it's confined to the male sex?

— I dunno, she says.

VIII

She is there waiting for him, at the same table, in the corner. The child is with her.

— This is Sophie, she says. Sophie's ballet class was cancelled, she explains. The teacher was knocked over by a rollerblader.

— Knocked over?

— On her way to school this morning.

— But she's all right?

— I guess so, she says. She just couldn't take the class today.

— Do you like the teacher? he asks the child.

— She's all right, she says.

— Sophie's going to go outside and play in a minute, Claude says. Aren't you, darling?

— I've heard a lot about you, Alan says to her.

The little girl turns and inspects him.

— Why don't you go out and play? Claude says. I'll order a juice for you.

— I don't want to play, Sophie says.

— Don't be tiresome, darling, her mother says.

— I'm not being tiresome.

— Do you want an ice-cream?

— No.

— Then what do you want to do?

— I don't know.

— Well, darling, if *you* don't know how am *I* supposed to?
The child is silent.

— Do you like your new school? Alan asks her.
She turns her gaze on him again.

— Well? her mother prompts her. Why don't you answer?

— No, she says.

— Why not?

— I don't have any friends.

— Well, you must make friends.

— I'm too old to make friends at my age.

— What did you say? Alan asks in surprise.

— Go on, darling, her mother says. Be a good girl.

— Do you miss your American friends? he asks.
She gazes at him in her disconcerting way.

— Go on, darling, her mother says. You know the sun's good
for you.

— I don't like the sun.

— There's a playground just across there, see?

— I don't like playgrounds.

— Don't be tiresome, darling, Claude says.

— What do you like? Alan asks her.

— Nothing.

— She misses her friends, Claude says.

— Why hasn't she made new ones?
Claude shrugs.

— We're very nice, Alan says to the little girl. Just as nice as

75

people in America, you know.

Claude takes her by the hand and leads her towards the door. — Just go outside and play in the sun, she says. Stay where we can see you.

— Where, Mom?

— Just out there, in the sun.

— I don't like the sun.

— Yes you do, Claude says. She pushes her outside and returns to the table. She's got to have sunshine, she says. Look how pale she is.

— Perhaps she's anaemic.

— No no. She needs to be in the sun more. There's not that much of it here, you need to catch it when it comes.

The child comes running back in, pulls down her mother's head and whispers in her ear.

— Tomorrow, Claude says.

— Promise, Mom?

— Promise. Now go and play, for goodness' sake.

— I'm sorry, Claude says when she has finally gone. She's not usually like this. The accident must have upset her.

— What accident?

— To the teacher.

— Of course. I forgot. But she wasn't hurt or anything, was she?

— No, but it must have been a shock to the children. She cranes her neck to see outside.

— She didn't want to come? he asks.

— Come where?

— Here. To England.

— No, Claude says. She was against it from the start. But you know what children are like.

76

— It didn't make you hesitate?

— It's good for her, Claude says. She'll thank me later in life. He calls the waiter and orders.

— You know what my mother always said? Claude says. She said parents couldn't win. Whatever they did would be wrong and held against them. So you might as well do what you want to do, no?

— I'll have to ask my mother whether that's what she thinks too.

— You see a lot of her?

— She's my best critic, he says. I always try out my ideas on her. She tells me at once if I've lost my way, gone off on the wrong track.

— It's funny, she says, you said exactly the same thing about her fifteen years ago.

— It was true then.

— What was it your professor wrote on the first piece you showed him? 'Avoid the editorial *we*'?

'*Eschew* the editorial *we*.'

— Yes. Eschew. Marvellous.

— You remembered? he says.

— I wish I'd been an academic, she says.

— That's funny, he says. We all wanted to be like you. A journalist. Involved in the real world.

— The real world! She snorts.

— That's how it seemed to us, he says. You and Byron. You seemed to know how to live. The rest of us only knew how to talk about books.

— How to live! Wow!

The waiter arrives with their tea.

— Tell me, she says. Did you enjoy the other evening?

77

— Didn't Sarah write?

— Of course she wrote. I'm asking you.

— You cook very well.

— I wasn't fishing for compliments. Besides, the meal was awful.

— It was good to see Byron, he says. Unchanged.

— Unchanged, she agrees.

He pours the tea.

— We shouldn't have asked the Susskinds, she says.

— Why?

— I don't feel it gelled, somehow. I thought you and Sam were very close.

— Not close, Alan says. I admire his energy.

— He has a lot for time for your work.

— Does he?

— He thinks you're the best.

— No he doesn't. He thinks he's the best.

— After him, she says, laughing.

He waits, watching her.

She stops laughing.

— Have a cake, he says, pushing the plate towards her.

— I won't today, she says.

— And the wolf?

— Do you remember the first time we met, Alain? she says.

— Uhuh.

— We began to talk in French, she says.

— *On pourrait toujours recommencer*, he says.

— *Pourquoi pas?* Except that my French has grown quite rusty since Mummy died.

— When was that?

— Five years ago.

— You miss her?

— I told you, she says. We didn't get on.

— But you miss her.

— Of course, she says. A parent takes part of one's life with them.

She reaches for the cakes. — I think I'm going to have one after all.

She chooses the chocolate slice.

— Where was she living?

— In Nice. Mad as a hatter.

— Why?

— How do you mean, why?

— How did it manifest itself?

— She stole hats out of hat-shops. And lived off tinned sardines.

— That seems quite sensible to me. I wouldn't mind ending up like that myself.

— Alain, she says, sometimes you say the most stupid things.

— Sorry, he says.

— I don't know why you do it.

— Neither do I, he says.

She eats, daintily, with her fork. He watches her.

— Alain, she says, why do I remember that period so intensely?

— I don't know.

— Do you?

— I don't know, he says.

— You must know, she says.

He is silent.

— That's another thing I remember about you, she says. You never minded saying you didn't know.

— Of course, he says. Why should one know everything? It's unnatural. But people keep thinking they have to be clear. I'm not clear about a lot of things, but that's all right. That's what I always tell my students: genuine puzzlement is much more productive than false clarity.

— Can't one get a little lazy and complacent with a doctrine like that? she asks.

He laughs. — *Touché*, he says.

— I didn't say you were. I thought it might encourage your students to become like that.

— It's better than coming up with clear and superficial answers every time.

— I wonder if your theory is not a little dangerous when applied to life and not to problems of the mind.

— Why do you say that?

— I don't know. I just wonder.

She starts to laugh. — You see, she says. It's infectious.

She pushes the plate away from her. — *Basta!* she says.

— Shall we see what Sophie's up to? he asks. And then take a stroll through the park?

Outside, the sun is shining and the child is sitting on a bench between two women, deep in conversation with them.

— Has she been pestering you? Claude asks them.

— Not at all, says one of the women, with a strong German accent. She has been telling us her sad story.

— What sad story?

— About the death of her parents in the car crash, the woman says. And how kind you have been to look after her.

Claude smiles at them.

— She is a lovely little girl, the other lady, also German, says. It is so sad.

— Yes, Claude says.

— Can I have an ice-cream now? Sophie asks from between them.

— No.

— Why, Mom?

— I asked if you wanted once before and you said no. Now we're going to take a walk.

— You have been so kind to her, the first lady says.

Claude holds out her hand. Reluctantly the child takes hold of it. Claude hauls her to her feet.

— It is tragic for a young child, the second lady says.

— Tragic, Claude agrees.

— Thank you for looking after her, Alan says, as he turns to follow.

— We did not look after her, the lady says. We only listen to her sad story. Such a lovely little girl.

Claude walks ahead, grim-faced, dragging her daughter by the hand.

— Mom! Let me go! she says. You're hurting me, Mom!

Claude lets her go. — Go on then, she says. Don't get lost.

He walks beside her, in silence, through the trees.

Finally she says: — I don't want to talk about it.

He walks beside her, hurrying to keep up.

— Not ever, she says.

The little girl disappears down a side-path.

— Is that clear? Claude says.

He takes her arm.

— Is it? she says.

— If you like, he says.

The little girl runs back to them, takes her mother's hand.
They walk.
— Don't drag on my arm, Claude says to her daughter.
— I'm tired.
— We're going home.
— I'm tired, Mom.
— We'll be at the gate soon, Alan says.
— I don't want to walk any more.
— Don't be tiresome, darling, Claude says.
They walk.
— There's the gate, Alan says.
— Are we going home? the little girl asks.
— Yes, darling.
— Can I have an ice-cream?
— No. We'll be having supper soon.
— And then can I watch a movie?
— We'll see.
— Mom, you promised!
— I have a headache.
— Oh, Mom, you promised! That's not fair!
— Here we are, Alan says, as they reach the park gates.
— You leave us here, Claude says to him.
— Are you sure?
— Absolutely. Goodbye.
— Goodbye, Alain.

IX

Now, it seems, they are sitting in Valerie's crowded patisserie in Soho.

— It's so difficult to know what to choose, he says. Perhaps one should make a point of coming here every day for a month and systematically try one cake after another. By the end of the month one would be able to make an informed choice — except that one would probably be so ill one would never want to see a cream cake again in one's life.

She eats her éclair, steadily, without looking up.

— How is Sophie? he asks. Has she got over the shock?

She puts down her fork and looks at him. — Alain, she says. What happened?

— What do you mean? he says.

— You know what I mean, she says.

He is silent.

— That day, she says, looking into his face.

— What day?

She picks up her fork again, toys with the remains of the cake, then pushes the plate away from her. — What happened,

Alain? she says, not looking at him.

He sips his coffee, watching her.

She looks at him again. — You've gone white, Alain, she says.

He looks away.

— What happened, Alain? she whispers.

He puts down his cup, spoons cream from the bottom.

— Alain, she says. Did you think I was dead?

He is looking at the tablecloth.

She waits.

Then she says again: — Did you?

She waits.

— Come, she says. It'll be easier walking.

Outside, on the pavement, she takes his arm.

— Perhaps it's not such a good idea, she says, as they are forced off the pavement for the third time by the surging crowds. Perhaps it would be easier if we sat down somewhere.

— Do you want us to go back to Valerie's?

— No. It was too crowded in there. And, actually, I didn't find the cakes that good.

— I was disappointed too, he says. It's gone down since I was last in there.

— What about this? she says.

They turn into the garden in Soho Square.

— There, she says, pointing to an empty bench.

They sit down. The sun is shining though the days are getting shorter.

She is silent, leaning back, looking up at the trees.

Finally he says: — Well?

She does not move.

He waits.

She speaks. — What did you think when you saw me? she says.

— When?

— At the Susskinds.

He is silent.

— You were scared, she says.

— Why scared? he asks.

After a while she says: — You don't know why I've come back. It scares you.

— Does it? he says.

She laughs. — Tell me what happened, she says.

He gets up. She leans forward, takes his hand. — Tell me, Alain, she says.

He sits again, his elbows on his knees, lets his head sink into his hands.

— Tell me, Alain, she says again.

He doesn't move.

She waits.

Above them, it seems, a helicopter drones in the greying sky.

Slowly he raises his head and looks at her. — It was a long time ago, Claude, he says.

— You thought I'd vanished for ever?

— Yes, he says.

She laughs.

— But you were waiting for me to appear, weren't you? she says. A part of you was waiting.

— Perhaps, he says.

She waits.

— Yes, he says.

She waits.

Suddenly she stands up.

— Where are you going? he asks, anxious.

— I've got to get back, she says. Sophie will be home from school.

— Already?

— Yes.

He holds his head in his hands, his elbows on his knees.

— Alain? she says gently.

He doesn't move.

She sits down on the bench again beside him. — Alain, she says, putting her arm round his shoulders.

— Alain, she says for the third time.

He raises his head and looks at her.

She throws back her head and begins to laugh.

He stares, but she goes on laughing.

— What? he says at last.

— I think it's very funny, she says.

— What is? What are you talking about?

— It doesn't matter, she says.

She gets up again.

She stands over him.

Finally she says: — I've got to go.

He sits, looking at the ground.

She turns abruptly and walks away from him. At the gate she stops and looks back. He stares after her.

She waits.

Then she turns and hurries off down the road.

X

— It's called *The Ghandian Ark*, Simon says. Only Utopian dreamers, ecologists and pacifists allowed on board.

Alan studies the painting in silence. Finally he takes a step forward and points: — Who's that? he asks.

— Schumacher.

— The racing driver?

— Of course not. The author of *Small is Beautiful*.

— I never read it.

— It made a big impact on me when I first came across it, Simon says. He had to be in there.

— And that one with the red beard?

— Lawrence of course.

— Of course. How silly of me.

— He's holding one of his paintings over his privates. The one that caused all the fuss.

— Yes, I see now.

They stand and look.

— What do you think? Simon asks.

— I don't know.

— You think the colours are wrong?

— No. I'm not sure anything's wrong. I just...

— I've been working on it for a long time, Simon says.

— I know. You've been talking about it for years.

— Not that it means very much, does it? Simon says. Sometimes the things that come quickly are the best.

— There's something about these very big canvases of yours, Alan says. I don't know. As if it's too much of a programme. Or is it just that it's not my scale?

— Yet you worship Rabelais.

— He's a miniaturist, really.

— Rabelais?

— You can write about giants but still be a miniaturist. You must think of him as a poet. Like Villon, whom he adores and quotes extensively.

— But all those lists, Simon says. All that food and shit and all the rest of it.

— If they printed each book of Rabelais' as a separate sixty-page volume you could carry in your pocket and take out to read a page of at intervals during the day everyone would see what I mean.

They look at the painting in silence.

— What was it Borges said? Simon says. Like all artists he judged others by their results and himself by his efforts.

— Aspirations, I think, Alan says. And himself by his aspirations.

— Even better, Simon says. It's good, don't you think?

— Too good. It hurts. Just remind me: Why ark?

— They're all those who tried to save modern civilisation. And now they're the only ones to survive the new flood.

— Why the only ones?

— Maybe they're not. Maybe it's a modern Ship of Fools. Shall we go and eat?

In the Flower of India Simon says, as he unfolds his napkin:
— Anything the matter? You look distracted.

— Do I?

— I think so.

— No. I'm fine.

— Your mother OK?

— Uhuh.

The waiter arrives. They order.

— I told you I met this woman? Alan says, when the waiter has gone. Out of my past?

— Cynthia?

— Claude.

— I thought it was Cynthia.

— No. Cynthia's someone else.

— What about her?

— Cynthia?

— No. Claude.

— I don't know. I can't get her into focus, somehow.

— How do you mean, into focus?

— I don't know.

The food arrives. As they help themselves Alan says: — I don't understand how I feel about her.

— You had a thing with her? Simon asks, biting into his poppadom.

— It was complicated.

— And you don't know whether to revive it?

— It's not like that.

They eat.

— She's reappeared in my life, Alan says, and it's as if I can't quite believe it's really her. It's as if it was someone saying she was so and so and –

– Because she's changed so much?

– No, on the contrary, because she hasn't changed at all.

– How long ago was it that you... Do you mind? he asks as he spears one of Alan's prawns.

– Of course I mind!

– Sorry. Sorry.

– Here. Have it.

– I just wanted a taste.

– Take the whole thing. I'm not really hungry.

– You've hardly eaten a thing.

– I'm not hungry.

– You're sure?

– Of course I'm sure. Go on. Have what you want.

– I will then, Simon says, pulling his friend's plate towards him. I didn't have any breakfast. Woke up late. Went straight down to the studio.

– I couldn't start the day without my breakfast.

– I grabbed a cup of coffee. But that's all.

Alan watches him.

– Are you in a hurry? he asks as he scoops up the last of the rice.

– I should be getting on. But it's fine. Don't rush.

– How long is it since you'd seen her? Simon asks, wiping his plate with a piece of naan.

– Fifteen years.

– And now she's turned up?

– Uhuh.

– She's pursuing you?

– No, it's not like that.

— Well what is it like then?

— I don't know. Come. Let's go.

In the street Simon says: — You want to talk about this woman?

— No no, Alan says. It'll sort itself out.

— You think so?

— Yes. I'm sure.

— Sarah know about it?

— About what?

— I don't know. This...

— There isn't anything.

— I'm just trying to understand, Simon says.

— She's met her. But it's got nothing to do with her.

— No?

— No, Alan says.

— Sorry, Simon says.

— Nothing to be sorry about, Alan says. I'll see you. Work well.

— And you. I never asked about the book.

— Another time.

— 'Bye.

— 'Bye.

XI

Now they are walking on Hampstead Heath.

– Tell me, Alain, she says. Tell me what happened.

He is silent.

They walk.

– Tell me, she says again.

– We were going to the sea, he says. We had eaten our picnic and we were going to the sea.

They walk.

– You were driving, he says.

– I was driving or you were driving?

– You were driving. It was your car and you were driving.

He is silent. They reach the ponds and stop.

– Go on, she says.

– You were driving. We were approaching the sea.

She begins to walk again. He catches up with her and they walk side by side.

– You told me to open the window, she says. You told me to open the window and smell the smell of the sea.

They walk.

— Go on, she says.

— I gave you directions, he says. You turned off the road onto a sandy path. You drove down it, getting ever closer to the sea.

He is silent.

— I told you to slow down, he says. I told you you were going too fast.

They walk.

— Go on, she says.

— You didn't pay attention, he says. The path twisted among the dunes. I told you to slow down.

— Go on, she says.

— Then you took a bend too fast and the wheels began to skid in the soft sand.

They walk.

— Go on, she says.

— There was no grip, he says. The car swung as you tried to control it and hit a stone.

— Go on, she says.

— No, he says.

— Go on, she says.

They walk.

— It was very still, he says. In the distance, I could hear the sea. Close to, a bird was chirping. Otherwise it was silent. You seemed to be asleep at the wheel.

They walk.

— Go on, she says.

— I called you, he says. You seemed to be asleep at the wheel.

They walk.

— I heard you, she says. I heard you calling.

— I got out of the car, he says. It wasn't easy. The door was jammed and I had to push to get it open. I wanted to be sick. But I couldn't. It wouldn't come. My stomach was churning but nothing came out. Only a bit of bile. I walked. The sea appeared over the dunes. I walked down to the sea. I sat.

They walk.

— Go on, she says.

He is silent.

— You left me there, she says. You left me in the car.

They walk.

— I sat on a stone, he says. I looked at the sea. I wanted to be sick.

He is silent, walking beside her.

— You left me there, she says again.

They walk.

— When I got back you had gone, he says.

He is silent, walking beside her.

— I thought I was dead, she says. When I came to I thought I was dead. It was very quiet in the car. Very quiet. Then I remembered. I called out, but you weren't there. I realised why it was so quiet: my watch had stopped.

They walk.

He waits for her to go on.

Finally he says: — I sat on a stone and looked at the sea.

He is silent.

— You left me there, she says. You didn't come back.

— I came back, he says. Eventually I came back. I thought I had mistaken the place because there was no car. I turned back to the sea. I looked round at the dunes. Then I saw the tyre marks.

— You left me for dead, she says. You could have called for help but you left me for dead.

— You were asleep, he says. I didn't want to wake you. I walked down to the sea. When I came back you had gone.

— You left me there, she says.

They descend into a wooded valley.

— No, he says. It was you who left me. I came back and you had gone. I saw the tyre marks where the car had skidded. And then where you had turned round and driven off.

— You didn't call, she says. In the days that followed.

— My father died, he says. I had to go back to England.

— You never called, she says.

— I sat by the sea, he says. I wanted to be sick.

— You knew I was dead, she says. You left me there knowing I was dead.

— You weren't dead, he says. You drove away and left me there. You turned the car and drove away.

— Yes, she says.

He is silent.

She says: — You got out of the car and left me. I could have been dead.

— I came back, he says. After a while I came back. There was no car.

— You saw the marks, she says. You saw the marks of the tyres. You could have called.

— You never looked for me, he says. You left me there and drove away.

She is silent.

— I found the tracks, he says, the marks of the tyres. There was no car. I couldn't believe you had driven off and left me there.

— I waited, she says. I waited and waited. Then I knew it was the end.

He is silent.

They emerge from the wood onto open ground.

— When I enquired they said you had gone, she says. Like that. Without a word.

— I didn't understand what had happened, he says. To me. To you. Then I had news that my father was dying. I came home.

— You left me there, she says. You left me for dead. You walked away from it and left me there. And then you left the country.

They walk.

— You wanted me dead, she says.

— No, he says.

— Then what? she says.

— I looked for the car, he says. I thought at first I had come back to the wrong place. In the dunes everything looks the same. And then I saw the marks of the tyres. Where we had skidded. Where you had turned. I began to walk. I found the road. I waited for someone to come by and give me a lift.

— You didn't come back, she says. I waited but you didn't come back.

They walk.

— Do you remember what we were talking about, Alain? she says. Before the car skidded. Before it hit the stone?

He is silent.

— Do you? she asks again.

— No, he says.

She takes his hand.

— Think, Alain, she says.

They walk towards the houses, the people.

XII

Now, it seems, they are walking through Epping Forest.
She is talking.

She says: — We took the car to the sea.

He walks beside her.

— We took the car to the sea, she says. My car. But you were driving.

She stops. He walks on, then returns to where she is standing.

She begins to walk again.

— I asked you to slow down, she says. But you paid no attention.

They walk.

— We came in sight of the sea, she says.

They walk.

— We came in sight of the sea and then it disappeared again, she says.

He walks beside her through the trees.

— You were driving along the sandy tracks, she says. I asked you to slow down but because we had quarrelled you wouldn't.

They walk.

— Go on, he says.

— You went round a bend, she says, and the wheels began to skid. Then the car hit a bank and started to climb. I remember, she says, I felt as though I was on a horse that was rearing up, and for a moment I thought it would go right over and I would have to protect my head somehow. I had never imagined that one might feel something like that in a car. I mean the slowness of it, the sense of it slowly rearing up and then falling over onto its back.

She walks.

Beside her, he says: — Go on.

— But it didn't, of course, she says. I must have hit my head on something, though, because I remember nothing else.

— Go on, he says.

They walk.

— I was lying in the sand, she says. It was dark. I thought I had gone blind at first, but then I realised I had my eyes tight shut. I tried to open them but there was blood trickling into them and I quickly closed them again. I wondered if I would be able to move.

He walks beside her. — Go on, he says.

The sunlight is filtering through the trees. She is walking beside him. — Go on, he says.

— I began to feel cold, she says. I thought I was dead.

They walk through the forest in the clear autumn air.

— I thought I was dead, she says again.

They walk.

— I opened my eyes, she says. It was dark. And then I heard the sea. I began to remember what had happened.

They walk.

— My head was hurting but I kept my eyes open, she says. I saw the sky, the stars.

He waits, walking beside her.

— I knew I would have to try and move, she says. I was afraid to. I was afraid I would find I couldn't. But it was easy. I rolled over. I sat up. Everywhere the silence. Except for the sound of the sea, on the other side of the dunes.

— Yes, he says.

— I looked round, she says. I waited, trying to see in the dark. Trying to hear. I was afraid of what I would hear.

— What? he says. Hear what?

— Blood, she says. Dripping. Or you moaning. Or, worst of all, nothing.

He waits. Then he says: — Go on.

She is silent.

Finally she says: — I got up and looked round. I could see the sea, now I was standing. A grey mass beyond the dunes.

— Yes, he says.

— I began to move, she says. Carefully at first because I could not see what was beneath my feet and I was not sure if I would be able to walk. I thought I would see you somewhere near me. And the car close by. But there was nothing.

— Perhaps you imagined it all, he says.

She is silent, walking beside him.

— Perhaps you have come here for nothing, he says.

— Perhaps, she says.

They come to a clearing in the trees. She stops. She speaks, not looking at him.

— I walked round, she says. In bigger and bigger circles. I couldn't understand why I couldn't find you. Or the car.

He waits.

— Then I sat down again, she says. I began to think. My right eye was hurting. My cheek was bleeding.

He waits.

— I thought: he has gone, she says. He has taken the car and gone. He has taken the car and left me there to die.

He waits.

Finally she says: — Do you remember why we were quarrelling? In the car? Laughing and quarrelling? Before I hit the bank?

He waits.

— I thought: the bastard, she says. He has taken the car and gone, leaving me here to die.

He waits.

— Leaving me here for dead, she says.

He waits.

Finally he says: — And then?

— I began to walk, she says. I began to walk away from the sea. My right eye had closed. My head was hurting. There was a moon. Not full. But enough to see by. I fell once or twice in the long grass of the dunes. My face was hurting. My shoulder and arm were hurting.

He waits.

— I walked in circles at first, she says. And then I found a track and tried to follow it. I lost it several times but I kept going.

He waits.

— It was like a dream, he says.

— Yes, she says. A dream.

He waits.

— And then? he says. And then?

— I came back to the place and the car had gone. You had gone. I didn't know what to do.

He waits.

— Then I began to walk, she says. I walked down to the sea. I walked over the sand through the long grasses to the sea.

He waits.

— I walked along the shore, she says. And then I realised I was lost. I walked and walked.

He waits.

— I came up from the sea, she says. I went back through the long grasses, the dunes. And then I saw the car. I got in and sat at the wheel. I waited. My head was hurting. The bleeding had stopped but everything was hurting.

She is silent.

— Go on, he says.

— That's all, she says.

They begin to walk again, through the trees, over the autumn leaves.

— You drove away, he says. You drove away and left me there.

— I sat in the car, she says. The keys were still in the ignition. I sat in the dark and waited.

— You drove away, he says. You turned the car and drove away.

She is silent. Then she says: — I waited. Day after day. Day after day. Then I heard you had left. Gone back to England. I was not surprised.

— My father was dying, he says.

— Yes, she says.

They walk.

— And then? he says.

— I decided to wait, she says.

— Wait for what? he asks.

— Wait, she says.

They walk.

— I knew I would, in the end, she says.

— Would what?

— Find you, she says.

She stops.

— Find me? he says. Why find me?

— You don't know? she says.

— No, he says. Tell me.

She takes his arm. They start to walk again through the trees.

— Tell me, he says.

— To kill you, Alain, she says.

They walk.

She begins to laugh.

— Yes? he says.

— You should see your face, Alain, she says. I wish I had a mirror. Just so you could see the face you are making.

He is silent.

— Do you really think I would want to kill you, Alain? she says.

He is silent.

— Do you think me capable of it, Alain? she says.

He is silent.

— Perhaps I am, she says. I don't know. Perhaps I am.

XIII

Now they are sitting in the Orangery once more. She has dark glasses on, though the winter has arrived.

— It's my eyes, she says.

— What happened?

— Nothing happened. My eyes have started hurting. I find it easier with the glasses on.

He pushes the plate of cakes towards her.

— No, she says, laughing. Not today.

— It's as bad as that?

She laughs.

He sips his coffee.

— Claude, he says. I've been thinking. It wasn't like that, you know.

— Like what?

— There was no accident, he says. The car skidded. It hit the bank and for a moment it seemed as if we were about to go over, but then it just came to a stop.

She sips her coffee.

— We sat in the car, he says. You switched off the engine. It was very still.

— Yes, she says. I remember.

— We didn't speak, he says. We were both shocked, I think, at what had happened. At what could have happened. We sat in the car. Then I got out. I came round to your side and opened the door. You didn't move. I left you and went and sat on a tuft of grass in the sand. After a while you came and joined me.

He is silent.

— Do you remember? he asks.

He looks at her. He cannot see her eyes.

— Yes, she says.

He pours himself another coffee.

— We sat in silence, he says, looking towards the sea. From where we were we could hear it, but not see it.

— Yes, she says. I remember.

— You lay back in the harsh grass, he says. You closed your eyes. After a while I stretched myself out beside you. We did not speak.

— Yes, she says. I remember.

— We lay in the harsh grass, he says. We could hear the sea in the distance. Otherwise there was no sound.

— Go on, she says.

— You fell asleep, he says. You fell asleep there beside me. I got up and went down to the sea.

— Go on, she says.

— I sat on the grass, where the dunes gave way to the beach, he says. I sat and looked towards the sea. Then I got up and began to walk.

He is silent.

— Go on, she says.

– I left you sleeping and began to walk along the shore, he says. When I got back you were gone.

He is silent.

– Go on, she says.

– I thought I had made a mistake, he says. I thought I had returned to the wrong spot. Then I saw the tyre marks. The marks where the car had skidded. And the marks where you had turned and driven away.

He stops.

She says: – When I woke up you were gone. I waited. My eye was hurting. There was blood on my face. I thought you had gone to look at the sea. Then I began to shiver. I got into the car. The key was still in the ignition. I sat and waited for you to return. Then I realised you had gone.

She stops.

He says: – Go on.

– I turned the key in the ignition to see if it would start, she says. And it did. Straight away. I thought the wheels would skid in the sand when I engaged the gear but it didn't. I turned and drove away.

She is silent.

Then she resumes. – I drove home, she says. The bleeding under my eye had stopped but my face was hurting like hell.

He waits.

After a while she says: – I waited for you to phone but you didn't. Then I heard you had left. You had gone back to England.

He is silent, looking at her across the table.

– Alain, she says.

– Take off your glasses, he says.

– You don't want to see my red eyes, she says.

— As you wish.

They sit.

— Claude, he says, why did you come back?

— Take me there, Alain, she says.

— There?

— Remember? You promised. At dinner. To take me to the sea.

— Yes, he says.

— Are you still up for it? she asks.

— Of course, he says.

— When?

— Soon, he says.

XIV

Now there is only the sound of their voices.

— That was not how it was, she says. You know that was not how it was.

Time passes.

Finally he says: — No?

Times passes.

He says: — Tell me.

He waits.

She begins. She says: — After a while we got out of the car. We were both shaken by what had almost occurred. We lay in the harsh grass. It was very cold. We lay, holding each other.

A time.

— Then, she says, we began to warm each other's bodies.

A time.

— You took off my clothes, she says.

He waits.

Finally he says: — And then?

— Oh, Alain, she says.

He waits.

— Alain. Alain, she says.

He waits.

— Take me to the sea, she says. I want you to take me to the sea.

— Yes, he says.

A time.

— I want to look at the sea with you, she says.

A time.

— I want to walk along the beach with you, she says. To listen to the tide sucking in the shingle, spitting it out, sucking it in, spitting it out.

A time.

— Will we go, Alain? she asks.

— Yes, he says.

A time.

— I took your clothes off, she says. Quite slowly. Do you remember?

A time.

— I was still in shock, she says. I needed to feel your body.

A time.

— Afterwards, she says, we went to sleep.

A time.

— Go on, he says.

— When I woke up you had gone, she says.

A time.

— Go on, he says.

— I thought you had gone down to the sea, she says. I covered myself with my jacket and went to sleep again.

A time.

— Go on, he says.

— When I woke up again you had not returned, she says.

A time.

— I began to feel cold, she says. I began to shiver. I put on my clothes and lay in the harsh grasses. You didn't come back.

A time.

— Go on, he says.

— I returned to the car, she says. I sat in the car and waited for you.

A time.

— Go on, he says.

— I waited but you didn't come back, she says.

— You didn't look for me? he asks. You didn't get out and look for me?

— Then I realised you had abandoned me, she says.

A time.

— Abandoned, he says finally. That's a big word.

— No, she says. It's not a big word. It's the truth.

A time.

— Go on, he says.

— I turned the key in the ignition to see if it still worked, she says. It did. I turned it off and waited.

A time.

— Go on, he says.

— When it became clear that you would not return I started the motor again, she says. Then I turned the car and went back the way we had come.

A time.

— Go on, he says.

— There's nothing more, she says.

— There's always more, he says.

A time.

— The sun came out, she says. You took off my clothes.

A time.

— Go on, he says.

A time.

He waits.

— Go on, he says.

— You went away, it seems she says. You left me naked and sleeping and you went away.

A time.

— Go on, he says.

— I waited, she says. When I got back home I waited for you to call.

A time.

— I waited for some sign from you, she says. But there was nothing. Then I heard you had left the country.

— Yes, he says.

A time.

— Go on, he says.

XV

Now he cannot see her. He cannot see her dark glasses, but he knows she is wearing them.

— Go on, he says.

— Come with me, Alain, she says. Come with me to the sea.

A time.

— Will you, Alain? she asks.

— Of course, he says.

A time.

— Go on, he says.

— We got out of the car, she says. We were shaken by what had almost happened. We lay in the harsh grass. Do you remember?

He waits.

— Go on, he says.

— You took off my clothes, she says. Very slowly. You took off my clothes.

A time.

— Then, she says, very slowly I took off your clothes.

A time.

He says: — Go on.

— Then you hit me, she says.

He waits.

— First you just bunched up your fist, she says. And you touched me, under the ribs, with your bunched hand. Then you pulled your hand back and hit me in the same spot. Not hard. As if you wanted to make sure I was really there.

A time.

— Go on, he says.

— No, she says. I can't.

He waits. Then he says again: — Go on.

A time.

— As if to make sure I was really there, she says. As though you wanted to impress my body on your mind. Then you hit me in the same spot, harder, and I cried out, and you hit me in the face.

A time.

— Go on, he says.

— I can't, she says.

He waits.

She begins to cry. In the dark. Beside him.

He waits.

The crying stops. He can feel her gathering herself.

He waits.

— I caught hold of your arm, she says. I bit it. Hard. Then you hit me again. You hit me in the eye. I could feel the blood on my tongue. Your blood. Or mine. I don't know. I managed to straddle you and I bit you again. You tried to push me away but I went on biting. That's when you dragged me over. You held me under you. You hit me and you hit me.

A time.

— Go on, he says.

— You remember, Alain? she says. How you hit me and you hit me?

He waits.

— Go on, he says.

— You went on hitting, she says. I thought it would never stop.

A time.

— Go on, he says.

— Finally you got up, she says. You left me for dead. You left me there in the harsh grasses in the sand by the sea.

A time.

He says gently: — Go on.

— I was sitting in the car, she says. My face hurt. My body hurt. My cheek was bleeding. I touched it and then I looked at my finger and it was covered with blood.

He waits.

— I sat in the car, she says. I don't know how I got there. But I was there. In the car. In the dark.

A time.

— Go on, he says.

— My body hurt from the ferocity of your attack, she says. From the pummelling of your fists.

A time.

— I haven't heard that word for a long time, he says: pummelling.

A time.

— I must have started the car, she says. I must have turned the car in the soft sand and driven away. I must have driven home through the night.

A time.

— My body hurt, she says. I had difficulty breathing. And the cut in my face kept bleeding. I held a handkerchief against it and I drove.

A time.

— Go on, he says.

But she is silent.

XVI

— I never see you any more, his mother says. Does that mean you're really getting on with your book?

— I wish it did, he says.

— How are the boys?

— Fine. Fine.

— I had a long talk with Adam the other day, she says. But they never come to see me.

— Let's not go into that again, Mum.

— All right. Tell me about your book then.

— Give me a cup of tea first.

— They used to do more than phone me up occasionally, she says, as she bustles about the kitchen.

— I told you, Mum, let's not go into that again.

She puts the cup down in front of him and sits down opposite, lighting a cigarette and drawing the ashtray towards her.

— So, she says.

— You're sure you want to hear?

— Of course I am. Get on with it.

— Well, he says, the question I'm asking myself is why

Rabelais should choose to present himself to the public under the name of Alcofribas Nasier, or, as he puts it on the title page of *Pantagruel*, his first book, 'Feu M. Alcofribas, Abstracteur de Quinte Essence' – the late Mr Alcofribas, Abstracter of Quintessence. What is the point of this anagrammatic pseudonym?

– Is that what it is? she says. An anagram?

– Uhuh.

She laughs, letting the smoke trickle out through her nostrils.

– He doesn't want people to know that he, a respected medical man, is writing bawdy nonsense, she says.

– Maybe.

– He's afraid of the censors. Afraid of getting into trouble with the authorities.

– Maybe.

– Go on then. Tell me.

– Nobody knows, of course, he says. But I suspect that the oddity of moveable type may have had something to do with it. The advent of print means the far wider dissemination of books. But it also cuts off the direct link between author and reader, which existed in the manuscript age. You –

– But weren't there scribes? she asks. Didn't they come between the author and his public?

– True, he says. But the scribe's task was to copy as faithfully as possible what the author had written. And for the reader the marks on the page were the marks left by a living hand. Or else the author read aloud what the scribe had copied, thus re-appropriating the material he had written. But in this new age of print words are decomposed into letters and the letters are anonymous. The author becomes nothing but a man who moves letters about and sets them down on the page – or gives instructions for others to do so. Just as you no longer have a stake in the tradition it turns out you are no longer a self either. *François Rabelais, Alcofribas Nasier* – what does it matter? There is not the stamp of either upon the text. It is only the spirit of the game, the spirit that will move letters around till they produce a striking word, a word redolent of magic – *Alcofribas*. Doesn't the name make you think of *abracadabra* and all the rest of it? But what of *Nasier*? Doesn't that make you think of *noses*, the least mystical of things? Alcofribas Nasier is the first example in our literature of the ironic juxtaposition of two registers in one unit, of which the most famous example is the title of Eliot's first major poem: 'The Love Song of J. Alfred Prufrock'. But here compressed into a single name. Two words only. I think that –

– You're going too fast again, his mother says. You've got to slow down if you're to take me with you.

– I'm sorry. Do you want me to try again?

– Yes, she says. Do you want another cup of tea?

– No thanks.

She lights another cigarette.

– The painter Phillip Guston once said something very nice about this, he says. He said that when he went into his studio everybody was in there with him: his dealer, the public, all the great artists of the past. They are all looking over his shoulder and talking. One by one they leave, and then he himself leaves, and then the painting begins.

His mother blows the smoke out through her nose, and, it seems to him, her ears.

– Take a man, any man, he says. Or woman. Filled with the desire to write, to speak to the world. But belonging to no circle of writers, like Ronsard. Without a patron, like du Bellay. Later in the century he will have a name: Montaigne. But this writer we are talking about has no belief such as Montaigne had that his thoughts could be of interest to anyone. They are certainly of no interest to him. What is he to do? Forget about this desire, perhaps, and plunge into his profession as a doctor? But what if the itch to write will not let him alone? It is like the itch to sing, to dance, but he is alone in his room and there is no one to sing with, to dance with, nothing but the blank page before him. So he begins to write, parodying the popular chapbooks of the time, but soon he finds that his book is taking off in an unexpected direction, with the introduction of the tattered and hungry figure of Panurge, *panourgos*, the cunning one, who, when asked who he is and what is the matter with him, speaks in every language under the sun except for his native one, French. And now the book is done and he must give it a title and an author. He feels himself to be more Panurge than Rabelais, but he is also Panurge's new master, Pantagruel. So who is he? Who was he as he wrote the book? In one mad moment he understands that who he was is none other than *the one who makes*, the one who has put the letters and words together. So he plays with the letters of his name, François Rabelais, tries out different patterns, as he had tried out different sentences in the course of writing his book, until he hits upon one which satisfies him, by its ludicrousness, its unlikeliness, and its nice combination of the magus and the fool. He puts down: ALCOFRIBAS NASIER. That is who the author of the book is. Not the doctor of medicine and wise humanist, François Rabelais, but this motley figure without a past and without a body, without even a soul, this figure who is only an agglomeration of letters. That, he feels, best expresses who the author of the book is.

He drinks down the cold tea at the bottom of his cup. – It

is nonsense to believe, he says, as some critics have, that there is no author of a text. Of course there is an author. But he is other than the man who lives in Montpelier and goes about his daily business of working, eating, and so on. He is someone and no one. He is the maker, the putter-together-of-letters. He is Alcofribas Nasier.

He stops. — Is that clearer? he asks.

— Not much, his mother says. There needs to be a lot more sorting out before you can be comprehensible to a lay person like me.

— You are my audience, he says. It is for you I write.

XVII

And now he is driving carefully through the streets of East London. She is slumped in the seat beside him.

— I can never believe this will actually end, he says. But it does. It always does.

He drives.

— Once, he says, when she was still driving, my mother got lost in the wastes of South London. She'd been to a play with a friend and had dropped her off and was trying to get back to her house in the country. It was about eleven or twelve at night. The streets were pretty much deserted and she was afraid. She was even more afraid when she found she was driving down a road she'd already been down fifteen minutes before. She was afraid to stop and consult a map and of course there wasn't a policeman in sight. So she kept on driving. At some point she got out of the loop and found herself on the right road out of London.

He drives.

— I hope the sun comes out, he says. It'll be pretty gloomy if it stays like this.

He drives.

— Though the sea looks good in any conditions, he says.

He drives.

— Alain, she says suddenly. Do you remember why you hit me?

He drives.

— Do you? she says.

— Yes, he says.

He drives.

— Why, Alain? she says.

— Because you asked me to, he says.

— No, she says.

He drives.

She says again: — No.

He drives.

— And before? he says. Do you know why we skidded? Why we almost had the accident?

He drives.

— Do you? he asks again.

She sighs.

— Tell me, he says.

He drives.

— Tell me, he says again.

— You were touching me, she says. You couldn't wait, could you, Alain?

He drives.

— No, he says. I couldn't wait.

He steers the car onto the motorway, speeding out of the city.

— It drove me mad, she says. I liked it so much it drove me mad. Your touching me like that.

He drives.

— I wanted it, she says. And I wanted you to hit me.

He drives.

— Yes, he says.

— Perhaps I wanted you to kill me, she says.

He drives.

— Is that right, Alain? she asks. I wanted you to kill me?

He drives. A thin mist envelops the car and he turns on the windscreen wipers.

— What were we thinking of, Alain? she says.

— I don't know, he says. I suppose we thought we were liberated.

She laughs and sits up straight. — Perhaps we were right, she says. Perhaps we've just become middle-aged and inhibited.

— Perhaps, he says.

— I took off my clothes, she says. Very slowly. Then I took yours off. You let me do what I wanted. I asked you to hit me, she says. You bunched your fist up and touched me. Just below the ribs. On the right. I closed my eyes and waited. Then you hit me. I wanted you to go on. And you did. You hit me and you hit me.

He drives, peering through the mist.

— You were afraid, she says. When you saw the blood you thought you'd killed me and you ran away.

He drives.

— You left me there, she says. In the sand. Deep in the harsh grass. You were afraid. You tried to pretend it never happened.

He drives.

— You never rang, she says. You were afraid they would say I was dead.

He drives.

He says: — I walked. I walked along the beach. I walked and I walked. Then I sat on a stone and listened to the sea.

— You didn't want to know, she says. You didn't want to think about it.

— Then I came back to the place where the car had been, he says. At first I thought I'd made a mistake. Lost my way. Then I saw the tyre tracks. Where we had skidded. Where you had turned the car round.

— You sneaked out of the country because you thought you had killed me, she says.

— When I came back you were gone, he says. I knew I hadn't killed you.

— Perhaps you came to the wrong place, she says. Perhaps they were not the marks of my car at all. Perhaps you didn't come back but kept on walking.

He drives.

— Perhaps you were afraid to go back in case I was there, she says. Dead. You walked away and tried to pretend it had never happened.

He drives.

— If you had killed me they would have got you, she says. Before you could have left the country.

— Of course, he says.

— So you knew I wasn't dead, she says. Yet you knew you had killed me. You knew you had killed me because I had asked you to.

He drives.

— Isn't that how it was? she asks.

— What does it matter? he says.

She is slumped beside him, pressed against the door.

She moans.

— Claude, he says.

He drives.

She appears to be asleep beside him.

He drives. He drives.

He opens the window: — Can you smell the sea? he asks.

She is asleep beside him.

— From the hotel, he says, one looks right out over the sea. There is the beach and then the sea. Nothing but the sea.

He drives.

— Claude, he says, are you asleep?

She opens her eyes, stretches.

— Where are we? she asks.

— We've arrived.

— Already?

— You were asleep.

He turns the car into the drive and loops round the big house to a car park at the back. He brings it to a stop, switches off the engine.

— Here we are, he says.

— Yes, she says.

He waits.

— Shall we go in? he says.

She sits beside him, silent, staring ahead of her.

He turns to look at her but she does not move.

— Alain, she says.

He waits.

Finally he says: — Come.

— Yes, she says.

He gets out of the car, stretches.

He goes to the back of the car, opens the boot, takes out the bags.

He goes round to her side of the car, opens the door. Come, he says again.

She sits, staring straight ahead of her.

— Claude, he says.

She gives him her hand. He helps her out.

— Ah, she says.

— What?

She does not look at him.

— What? he says again.

She bends and picks up her bag. She begins to walk towards the door of the hotel.

He hurries to catch up with her. He takes her arm.

— Claude, he says.

She stops.

— Do you want to do this? he says.

She puts down the bag, stands, waiting.

— We can go back, he says.

He lets go her arm. He waits.

She bends stiffly, picks up the bag again.

— Claude, he says.

— Oh, Alain, she says. Don't be so silly.

— Silly? he says. Why?

— Why? she says. Because we're here. It's too late to go back now.

— No it isn't, he says.

She waits, holding the bag.

— We can still go back, Claude, he says.

— To what? she says.

— To what we were before.

— Before what?

— Before now.

— There's only before then, she says. And we can't go back to that.

She picks up her bag again and marches up the steps. He follows her into the hotel.

XVIII

As they are eating the fish course she twines her ankles round his under the table.

She says: — I want to go out.

— Now?

— When we're done.

— It's dark.

— I want to walk along the beach in the dark.

— You want to go alone?

She is bent over her food.

He repeats: — Alone?

— No, she says, not looking up. With you.

She finishes, lines up the knife and fork on her plate.

— What are you thinking? he asks.

— Nothing, she says.

The waiter takes away their plates.

— I want to hear the shingle being sucked away by the tide, she says. Sucked away and thrown back, sucked away and thrown back.

He watches her.

The waiter serves the next course.

He eats.

She grips his ankles under the table.

— Wait, she says, as she feels him wriggle.

— For what? he says.

She laughs.

And now they are eating their dessert.

She eats, not looking at him.

She licks the spoon like a child.

He waits, watching her.

She licks the spoon, dreaming.

She puts down the spoon suddenly on her empty plate, looks round the room. — Right, she says.

They get up, push their chairs back in under the table and leave the half-empty room.

Inside the bedroom he tries to hold her but she slips away from him.

She goes into the bathroom. He stands at the window, looking out at the darkening sea.

When she comes out he looks at her in surprise. — You've put your hair up, he says.

She smiles, her face white.

— I've never seen you with your hair up, he says.

— Now you have, she says. Ready?

— One sec, he says, and goes into the bathroom.

When he comes out she has gone.

He calls out: — Claude!

Silence.

He walks round the room, stands at the window.

He steps out into the corridor. He calls again, low: — Claude?

He walks to the top of the staircase.

An elderly couple is coming up the stairs. He smiles at them.
— Good evening.

They nod to him and go off along the corridor, the man fumbling for his keys.

He goes back into the room and looks round again, goes to the window again, gazes down at the deserted beach and the sea, silvery now in the moonlight.

He goes to the door again, opens it, goes down the corridor and starts to descend.

At the bottom he peers into the now deserted dining-room. A waiter comes towards him: — Can I help you sir?

— No thanks, he says quickly, and retreats.

He returns to his room, takes his coat and goes out, locking the door behind him.

Outside the hotel he hesitates, then walks down to the sea. When he reaches the edge of the water he turns to the right and begins to walk.

He walks, keeping close to the sea, where the shingle gives way to pebbles and patches of wet sand.

Clouds have covered the moon and it is quite dark now.

He walks. As he walks he calls: — Claude? And then, more loudly: — Claude?

He turns and looks back the way he has come. The beach appears to be deserted.

He begins to walk back, his feet crunching the tiny shells the tide has thrown up.

He passes the hotel and stops, looking up to the room where he has left the light on. Nothing moves in there.

He goes on walking.

The clouds have thinned and the moon is struggling to get out.

He walks.

The last buildings have given way to dunes now. He stops again and looks back at the way he has come.

The beach still seems to be deserted.

He turns and faces the sea.

Far out, in the distance, a line of silver runs across the dark waters.

He begins to walk again.

A light wind has arisen, and he buttons up his coat.

He walks.

On his right, the sea. On his left, the dunes.

The moon suddenly increases in brightness and the line of silver spreads over the waters.

He stops and turns away from the sea, towards the dunes.

He stands, looking.

At the edge of the dunes he thinks he can make out a figure, standing, watching him.

— Claude? he calls out.

He begins to walk towards her.

She has not moved and he stops again, unsure of what he is seeing. — Claude? he says again.

The figure, if it is a figure and not a bush, stands quite still.

He advances a few steps and stops once more.

— Claude? he says again.

He hurries over the shingle towards the dunes. The figure has vanished.

— Claude? he calls out. Are you there?

He has left the beach now and engaged with the sand and harsh grass of the dunes.

— Claude? he calls. What happened?

He stops again and listens. The only sound is the steady

breathing of the tide.

He stumbles and finds himself in a sandy hole. He climbs out, tugging at the rye grasses for support.

– Claude? he calls out. Are you there?

He stands on a hillock and looks around.

The moon emerges again and abruptly lifts the veil off the landscape.

Behind him, the steady breathing of the sea.

Around him, the silent dunes.

– Claude? he calls again.

And then he sees her.

He starts to walk towards her, over the dunes.

XIX

— It's basically concentrating on Ashbery and Heidegger, the woman with the green hair says. It's to do with the infra-ordinary, as I like to call it, and with the limits of language. Of course, she says, I'm only dealing with the later Ashbery, the work that comes after the *Convex Mirror.*

— Excuse me, Alan says.

— I haven't finished, the woman with the green hair says.

— I realise that, Alan says, but I need to pee.

— In that case, the woman says, you'd better go.

He looks for Sam Susskind in the crush.

— Well well, a voice says in his ear. The man with the footballing sons.

He turns and smiles at her. — How is your mother-in-law?

— How do you know my mother-in-law?

— Don't you remember? We met on Hampstead Heath. You were off to see your mother-in-law.

— So I was. We had a little flirtation.

— I wouldn't call it that, Alan says.

— You wouldn't? she says. How disappointing.

— I'm looking for Sam Susskind. I'm sure he must be here somewhere.

— Yes, she says. I saw him a moment ago. Try the kitchen.

— Thanks.

— Won't you stay and talk to me first? she asks, flashing her full-lipped smile at him.

— I'd love to but I can't. I have to speak to Sam.

— You have to?

— Perhaps I can come and find you later? When I've spoken to him?

— Perhaps, she says. Who knows?

The kitchen is empty but in the hall he finds Ronnie Chinn.

— You said you'd come and see me again, Ronnie Chinn says.

— I'm sorry. I haven't had a moment. You know what it's like when you're on leave.

— No, Ronnie Chinn says. I'm a lawyer. We don't have leave.

— It's just that one gets desperate not to waste it. So one rushes around trying to make sure one won't have to rush round any more for a while and one can get on with one's work. I know that sounds cockeyed but... I'm looking for Sam Susskind, actually.

— I don't know why I came, Ronnie Chinn says. I don't really want to talk to anyone.

— I'm sorry, Alan says. Is it still bad?

— On the other hand I can't bear to be by myself, Ronnie Chinn says.

— You haven't seen Sam Susskind then?

— I haven't seen anyone, Ronnie Chinn says. Not anyone I know. Except you. I don't know why I came.

— I have to find him, Alan says. I'll see you.

He finds Sam Susskind in the library, deep in conversation with a tall, white-haired, cadaverous-looking man.

— This is Arnold Lewis, Sam Susskind says, extending an arm and drawing Alan to him. This is Alan Schneider.

— Good to meet you, Alan, Arnold Lewis says. You'll bear it in mind, won't you? he says to Sam Susskind.

— Sure.

— Any queries, don't hesitate to call.

— Sure.

— Good to have met you, Alan, Arnold Lewis says, shaking hands all round.

— And you, Alan says. I've been looking for you everywhere, he says to Sam Susskind when the other has gone.

— What can I do for you?

— What happened to Claude?

— You don't know? She's gone home.

— Home? Where?

— Cambridge, Mass.

— She's gone home?

— That's what I said.

— I thought they were here for the year?

— Byron's stayed.

— But she and Sophie have gone back?

— Uhuh. Byron's here somewhere. You haven't seen him?

— I can't believe this, Alan says. Do you know why she went?

— Apparently Sophie wasn't doing too well at school. She was being bullied and hated it and Claude thought it would be best to take her back.

— You mean she's been planning this for some time?

— Just the last few weeks, Sam Susskind says. I can't

134

remember when she actually decided.

He takes a sip of his drink. – Pity, really, he says.

– What do you mean?

– What did you think of her?

– How do you mean?

– What did you think of her? How did you find her after all these years?

– Good, Alan says.

– Pretty good, Sam Susskind says.

– What do you mean?

– Generous with it.

– I don't understand.

– Do I have to draw you a diagram? Sam Susskind says smiling, his even white teeth gleaming.

Alan stares at him. Sam Susskind's smile broadens.

– I don't believe it, Alan says.

– Mind you, I don't think I was the only one, Sam Susskind says. In fact, at one point I even thought that you...

– You're kidding me, Alan says.

– Why should I want to do that?

– She's gone back? Like that?

– Like what?

– I mean...

– Yes, Sam Susskind says dreamily. I'll miss her. I'll definitely miss her.

– You're pulling my leg, Alan says. Tell me you're pulling my leg.

– I'm pulling your leg, Sam Susskind says.

– Thank God for that.

Sam Susskind smiles at him.

— You are, aren't you? Alan says.

— What?

— Pulling my leg.

— No. Of course not.

— Then why did you say you were?

— You asked me to.

— I asked you to? What are you talking about?

— You said: Tell me you're pulling my leg. So I did.

— But you weren't?

Sam Susskind shrugs.

— She decided to go back weeks ago? Alan says.

— I don't know if it was weeks, Sam Susskind says. At this stage of the term everything kind of rushes by, if you know what I mean.

— I see, Alan says.

— She owes you money? Sam Susskind asks.

— No no. Nothing like that.

— Then what? You had something going between you?

— No, Alan says. Just the past.

— It doesn't do to dwell on the past too much, Sam Susskind says. That's what I've always found, at least. It's a bit of a dungheap, if you ask me. Look forward, as my old man used to say. Forward and upward. Then you can't go wrong.

— Bit of a joker, was he, your old man? Alan asks.

— Not really, Sam Susskind say. More of a realist, I'd say. Hey, he says. I've got myself a new set of teeth. Want to see them?

Making Mistakes

If it could have been otherwise, it would have been otherwise.

Franz Kafka

I

Dorothy is just in the process of serving the fruit salad when the phone rings.

— Damn, she says.

— I'll answer, Tony says, picking the phone off its rest on the sideboard and going out into the corridor.

— One ought really to switch off all phones when one has friends round, Dorothy says. Just like the theatre.

— I wouldn't ever do that, Deirdre says. What if there's an emergency?

— Emergencies can wait, Dorothy says.

— I know what you mean, Henrietta says to Deirdre as Dorothy, having served her guests, sits down again. When Nigel's away if I have to put oil in my ears or something like that I'm terrified I won't hear the phone ring in case it's an emergency.

— What a peculiar thing to do, Dorothy says, to put oil in your ears.

— You have to, periodically, if you get wax in your ears as Hetty does, Nigel says.

Tony re-enters the room. — It's your sister, he says to Dorothy.

— What does she want?

— To come and stay.

— Come and stay?

— She's leaving Charlie.

— Again?

Tony shrugs and sits down at the table. He helps himself to fruit salad.

— I hope you said we couldn't have her, Dorothy says.

— She's just packing her things, Tony says.

— We can't have her, Dorothy says.

— She'll be round in an hour or two, Tony says. He pours cream on his fruit salad. She's only going to stay till she finds somewhere to live, he says.

— An hour or two? Dorothy says. I can't believe this. Give me the phone.

— She's made up her mind, Tony says.

— She'll have to unmake it.

— She said she was glad it was me she was talking to. She said I'd understand. She said she was switching off her phone in case you tried to ring and dissuade her.

— I can't believe what I'm hearing, Dorothy says.

— She's leaving her husband, Tony explains to their guests. She says she can't take any more.

— What can't she take? Henrietta asks.

— Is she leaving the children with him? Deirdre asks.

— My sister, Dorothy says, is the most irresponsible person I have ever met.

— Come come, one doesn't meet one's sister, intervenes Alfonso, who has been quiet so far.

Dorothy swivels in her chair and stares at him.

— Is she leaving the children with him? Deirdre asks again.

— How many children do they have? asks Henrietta.

— Three, Tony says.

— Have some more fruit salad, Dorothy says. Hetty?

— I will have a little more, Henrietta says. What did you put in it?

— Mango, Dorothy says. Passion fruit. Melon. Orange. And guava.

— I don't think I've ever had guava, Henrietta says. What does it look like?

— You haven't had guava? It's got the most divine smell. The smell's almost better than the taste.

— And what does it look like?

— Nothing much, really, Small and roundish and a sort of dirty yellow. I'm sure your man in St John's Wood has some.

— She didn't say anything about the children, Tony says.

— My sister, Dorothy says, is the most irresponsible person I have ever met.

— She does have rather a lot to put up with, Deirdre says.

— Why? Henrietta asks.

Deirdre helps herself to some more fruit salad.

— Why? Henrietta asks again.

— Her husband, Tony says, is carrying on with a woman he met in a hat shop.

— A hat shop?

— Half his age.

— Half his age?

— She works in a hat shop? Nigel asks.

— Exactly, Dorothy says. A woman half his age who works in a hat shop. Angie.

— Angie?

— She's trying to finish a Ph.D, Tony says.

— Ph.D! Dorothy says. She's a sexual predator.

— There are plenty of sexual predators trying to finish their Ph.Ds, Alfonso says.

— What are you trying to say? Dorothy says.

— Nothing, I was just pointing out that you don't have to be *either* a sexual predator *or* a Ph.D student.

— And what's that supposed to mean?

— It's in art history, I believe, Tony says. Something to do with Poussin.

— Everybody at the Warburg is obsessed with Poussin, Henrietta says.

— It's the Blunt influence, Nigel says.

— What you have to understand about my sister and her husband, Dorothy says, is that they are both extremely weak people. Don't get me wrong. They are extremely likeable. Charming even. But weak. Neither has ever been able to say no. As a result they lurch from one crisis to the next, from one tearful scene to the next, from one decision to reform to the next, until in the end they wouldn't know how to live in any other way, even if they could.

— So before there was Angie there was Sissy, and before there was Sissy there was Prue, and before there was Prue there was La-La. And Bea for her part almost ran off with Colin and then with Alan and then with Francis, Tony says.

— But none of it ever means anything, Dorothy says. Perhaps it did at first, but not any more. I'm not passing judgement, she says. How could I? I'm human too, aren't I? I'm just putting you in the picture.

— So she rings Dot, Tony says, and she comes round and

144

she cries a lot, and then she goes home and they make it up.

— I know the part luck plays in these things, Dorothy says. Don't get me wrong, I know how lucky I am to have found Tony and how easy it is to try and tell other people how to live their lives.

— Dot doesn't say very much, Tony says, but it's as if having a sympathetic ear in which to pour out her woes does Bea good. A day or two with us and she's usually ready to return home.

— Excuse me, Dorothy says, but I'm fed up with being a sympathetic ear. I love my little sister dearly, she says to the others, but I really cannot stand weakness. I cannot stand people who don't know their own minds. They make me want to scream.

— You never show it, Tony says.

— Of course I don't show it, Dorothy says. I was brought up to think of politeness as something more than a social veneer.

— This thing with Angie has been going on for much longer than any of the others, Tony says. He doesn't seem to be able to break with her.

— He's starting to feel old, Dorothy says. He's starting to feel he may be in the last chance saloon.

— There are times, Tony says, when I feel really sorry for him. He is bored and miserable at home and he flies to this Angie and then he realises she's a nut case and he flies back home.

— What you don't understand, Dorothy says, is that he likes this kind of life. He likes the deceits and the hysteria and the rest of it. And so does she.

— I feel I have to intervene here, Alfonso says. After all, you were both once intimately bound up with them.

— What on earth do you mean? Henrietta says.

— More fruit salad anyone? Dorothy asks, and when they say no she begins to gather up the plates.

— What on earth do you mean? Henrietta repeats.

— How long have you known these people? Alfonso asks.

— Five, six years, Nigel says.

— The events I am talking about happened some fifteen years ago, Alfonso says.

— You've known each other that long?

— Deirdre was at university with them, Alfonso says.

— You knew each other at university?

— She knew them and she knew Bea and Charlie. Then when Deirdre and I met in graduate school I got to know them too. The two sisters, Dorothy and Beatrice, and the two friends, Tony and Charlie.

Dorothy serves the coffee.

— You and your sister were at Oxford together? Henrietta asks her.

— No. I was at Oxford and she was at Bristol. But she would come and stay with me.

— But Tony and Charlie were at Oxford?

— Yes, Tony says. We were at the same college.

— What you have to understand, Alfonso goes on, is that in those days Tony went out with Beatrice and Dorothy with Charlie.

— You don't say! Henrietta says. Really?

— Ask them, Alfonso says, stroking his beard and smiling.

Tony shrugs, feeling their gaze upon him. They look round for Dorothy but she has left the room.

— Didn't just go out, Alfonso says. They were actually engaged.

— Both couples?

Alfonso busies himself with his coffee. — Both couples, Deirdre says.

— Why don't you get to the point? Tony says.

— He's always been in a hurry, Alfonso says to the others. Remember what Kafka said? Because of impatience they were expelled from paradise; because of impatience they cannot return.

Dorothy takes her place at the table again, reaches out for the coffee pot.

— Spare us the sententiae, Tony says.

Alfonso cocks a finger: — Ah, he says, Pavlov strikes again.

— Why Pavlov?

— I mention university and he starts to speak Latin. His fingers play about his mouth: — Like those dogs of Pavlov's salivating at the ringing of a bell.

Dorothy hands round the chocolates Nigel and Henrietta have brought.

— Go on, Henrietta says. You were telling us about them being engaged to each other.

— You know how it is when you're young, Alfonso says. You want to make the world conform to your desires. After the indecisions of adolescence, with its monstrous sense that you are drifting on still waters in a rudderless boat —

— God, Tony says.

— In a rudderless boat, Alfonso repeats, what you long for is a great, all-consuming love that will redeem you, that will give a meaning to your existence and allow you to live in peace and joy for the rest of your life. That was how these two couples loved each other. Each had found in the other the fulfilment of his or her dream, Tony with Beatrice and Charlie with Dorothy. I tried to bring a little sanity into the situation. After all, I come

147

from a different culture, where reason and prudence play a big part in one's choice of partner —

— Thank you very much, Deirdre says.

— No no, Alfonso says, it is you I have to thank, my darling. In her, he explains to the others, I found a woman who was not only beautiful and wise but witty and commonsensical at the same time. Not to speak of wealthy. Since it was clear to me even then that only by a stroke of great good fortune would I ever again be able to chance upon such a paragon, I of course immediately proposed to her and, to my delight, she accepted me.

— I'll give my version of events later, Deirdre says.

— However, Alfonso says, I have to say that I was concerned for my friends Tony and Charlie. I did not feel that they approached the question with the kind of common sense that is required. Contrary to popular belief, it is the English and the Americans who are much the most romantic, the most idealistic lovers, perhaps because of the Puritanism so deeply embedded in the culture, which makes them feel that physical desire is evil unless it is accompanied by profound sentiments. Tony here and his friend were typical products of a certain English culture and upbringing. And here they were, at the age of twenty-three, determined to marry two charming sisters, which might seem like an admirable thing to do, but I, as their friend, felt that they nurtured unrealistic expectations of their future spouses, which might, in the long run, lead to a great deal of unhappiness. I decided therefore to conduct a little experiment. I intimated to Tony that Dorothy, as well as her sister, was not immune to his charms, and to Charlie that Beatrice, as well as her sister, was not immune to his. And I persuaded Deirdre to sow similar seeds in the minds of the two young women.

— We were *very* young, Dorothy interposes.

— You were twenty-two and twenty-three years old respectively, Alfonso says, but a French or Italian, a Mexican or Indian twenty-two-year-old is a good deal more mature than an English twenty-two-year old. Anyway, he says, twenty-two and twenty-three is what you were, and what your young men were, and at that age – perhaps at any age – one is rather pleased to be informed that one is attractive to an attractive member of the opposite sex, even if she is your beloved's sister or best friend. May I have another cup of coffee?

Dorothy pours him a second cup and glances round the table enquiringly. Deirdre pushes her cup forward but the others shake their heads.

He takes a sip and continues: – Having stirred at least a little interest in one who was not their beloved in the breast of each, I proceeded to the second stage of my plan. I found the opportunity to speak to each of the men on his own and I put it to him that since they were likely to pass a good deal of their lives in the company not just of their spouse but of her sister, and that the temptation to stray, given that each did not find the other unattractive, was highly likely to occur, it might be better to give it a try before rather than after they had pledged their troth to each the other. If they found that it was so good they could not do without it they were in time to switch their affections without causing untold damage. And Deirdre put the same proposition to the girls. Now although two in particular protested that they would never dream of doing such a thing, that the danger of hurting their beloved was too great a risk to take, they were eventually all won round.

— You went ahead? Henrietta asks, gazing with big eyes first at Tony and then at Dorothy.

Tony shrugs while Dorothy looks down at the table.

— What happened?

— Well, Alfonso says, Tony arranged to take Dorothy away for the weekend without either Charlie or Beatrice knowing and they in their turn arranged a little tryst without the knowledge of the others.

He reaches out for the box of chocolates, selects one after much hesitation, and puts it in his mouth. The others wait, watching him.

— And then? Henrietta says, when he shows no sign of wanting to continue.

— As you might expect, he finally says with a smile, the two occasions were an utter disaster. All four were far too conscious of what it was they were doing, far too riddled with guilt and embarrassment really to enjoy it. They returned to their respective lovers with a sigh of relief.

— I don't understand, Nigel says. Dorothy here returned to Charlie and Tony to Beatrice?

— Precisely. And both couples decided there and then to bring forward the date of their marriage, secure now in the knowledge, which, after all, had been tested, of their love for each other. I could not have asked for a better outcome to my little experiment.

— I still don't understand, Nigel says. How come then that Tony and Dorothy...?

— Ah, Alfonso says, that is the beauty of life, is it not? That we never know where it is going to take us.

He looks round the table with a smile.

— Well? Henrietta says. Go on.

— You see, he says, human beings are complex creatures. We think we know ourselves and then suddenly, hey presto! we find we don't. While the wedding preparations were in progress and our lovers were absorbed in their dreams of a future bliss, Tony took a train to Devon. He felt the need to be by himself at this most important juncture of his life, and to try and bring a little order into his mind, which it would not be amiss to describe as in turmoil. He booked a room at a little seaside hotel a friend had recommended and spent his time going for long walks along the cliffs and beaches of that delightful region. Though the weather was glorious and the scenery unparalleled he was disappointed to find that it failed in its purpose, which was to bring peace to his heart and clarity to his mind. After two days he decided that there was no point in staying any longer and returned to London. On the way he rang Dorothy and asked if he could have a word with her, and as soon as he arrived, not even giving himself time to go home and leave his bags, he went round to her place. She was waiting for him and offered him a cup of tea. They sat in her kitchen and while she was making the tea he told her that he had a problem. In the course of the past few days it had become clear to him, he said, that he was in love not with Beatrice but with her, and he wondered what she thought he should do about it. May I?

He reaches forward and draws the box of chocolates towards him. He studies the diagrams on the lid for a while, then examines the contents of the box. Finally he pulls out a chocolate and puts it in his mouth.

— Is this true? Nigel asks his hosts.

Tony shrugs, as if to say: Take it or leave it.

Alfonso swallows the last of the chocolate and resumes. — She told him, he says, that that was entirely up to him, that she wondered why he had come to her with his problems.

They look at Dorothy. — I think one has responsibilities,

she says suddenly and a little too loudly. We are not animals.

— He asked her to think about it, Alfonso says. He explained to her that a great deal depended on her decision She asked him to elaborate. He said that if she did not reciprocate his feelings he would have to do one of two things: break off his engagement and leave the country, or go ahead with his marriage in the knowledge that he did not and never could love his wife, that, worse, he loved her sister and the wife of his best friend. She replied that only he could make that kind of decision, and she did not know why he was burdening her with it. Dorothy, he said to her, you have not told me what you feel about me, and that gives me a kind of hope. I do not see what my feelings have to do with it, she replied. You would marry someone you didn't love? he asked. One can grow into love, she replied, and that is the answer I should have given to your question about what you should do.

— We are not animals, Dorothy says again, a little too loudly. There is such a thing as a duty to others and to one's word.

Alfonso goes on: — I take the answer to my question is no? Tony enquired. What is your question? she asked. Will you marry me? he said. I have told you, she said, we are not animals, we have our human responsibilities. Seeing that he was not going to get anything more out of her that day, Alfonso says, but nevertheless buoyed to some extent by her refusal to say outright that she cared nothing for him, he got up to leave. I have one thing more to say to you before I go, he said. It is this. Your response just now, and right through this painful scene, only serves to make my feelings for you more powerful. In this day and age, he said, when the whole of the Western world has lost all religious feelings, where people drift aimlessly on a sea of conventional emotions, you don't know how it lifts the heart to find a woman of principle. I don't have principles, Tony, she replied. Like all of us I only do what I feel will make me happy. That is what I mean, he said. Your notion of happiness is pure, that of the rest of the world is tainted. And with that he left.

Alfonso stops talking and beams at them. — That is the end of the story, he says.

Tony shrugs.

— Oh come on, Henrietta says. You can't stop there. What happened next?

Now it is Alfonso's turn to shrug, though he does it with more panache than Tony.

— Come on, Henrietta says, turning first to Tony and then to Dorothy. You can't stop there. You've got to tell us what happened.

— You know what happened, Deirdre says. Alfonso is right to stop there.

— *You* know what happened, Henrietta says. But we don't.

— Yes we do, darling, Nigel says. Dorothy married Tony and her sister married Charlie.

— But they weren't in love! Henrietta exclaims.

— How do you know that?

— Well, they were going to marry the other ones!

— It's amazing how quickly we human beings can persuade ourselves of something, Alfonso says. We need to find a story to support our feelings, of course, but the story Charlie and Beatrice told themselves and each other can easily be imagined. After all, as I said earlier, life has a strange way of taking us where we did not expect to go.

— But did you...? Henrietta asks Dorothy.

Dorothy smiles. — It was a long time ago, she says.

— You understood that...?

— It was a long time ago.

— But I want to know if you actually...?

— Darling, Nigel says, I think we should be going,

— So should we, Deirdre says, getting up.

Alfonso smiles at her, stroking his beard.

As they make their way to the hall and the coats Nigel says to him: — You weren't just... telling a story, were you?

— Of course, Alfonso says, smiling.

— None of it's true?

— Of course.

— Of course it is or of course it isn't?

— Of course it is.

— True?

— As true as a story can be.

— Don't let him tease you, Deirdre says as Alfonso helps her into her coat.

— I won't, Nigel assures her.

— Thank you so much, Henrietta says at the door to Tony and Dorothy. I was so touched to hear your story.

— Were you? Tony asks.

— What do you mean?

He shrugs.

Nigel places Dorothy's hand between his two. — My dear, he says.

— My friends, Alfonso says, embracing first Tony and then Dorothy.

Deirdre embraces them in turn and then follows the others out into the night. Tony stands at the door, waving until they are out of sight.

154

II

Dorothy has already started clearing the table.

— Well, Tony says, what did you think of that?

— I hope she isn't going to arrive too late, Dorothy says.

— Oh God, he says, that little scene had quite driven it from my mind.

They are well used to the rituals of washing up after a dinner party. Tony is already at the sink, his sleeves rolled up, rinsing out the plates and stacking them in the machine, while Dorothy is busy shaking out and folding the tablecloth and restoring the room to its normal appearance.

— Ten to twelve, Dorothy says. It's a bit much, don't you think?

— Perhaps she didn't want to make an appearance in front of our guests, Tony says.

— So she's going to keep us up till two in the morning? Dorothy says. Doesn't she know we've got a child asleep upstairs?

— It's a delicate line, Tony says.

— You bet it's delicate, Dorothy says.

Then the phone rings.

Dorothy picks it up and walks out of the room, closing the door behind her. Tony rinses the plates and stacks them in the machine.

— Well, that's sorted out, Dorothy says, re-entering the room and returning the phone to its cradle.

— What is?

— She's not coming.

— She's found somewhere else?

— No. They've made it up.

— Oh my God, Tony says.

— You knew it would happen, she says.

— Yes, but not so quickly.

Dorothy and sits down at the table. Tony gets to work on the saucepans.

— I have nothing against her leaving him, Dorothy says. In fact I think it would be a good idea, though how she would cope with three children on her own is another question. But what I can't stand is this constant shilly-shallying, this daily drama.

— That's their life, Tony says.

— I know it's their life, she says, But I can't stand it. I can't even stand being on the sidelines and looking on. It gives me the shivers.

— You don't have to look on, he says.

— Of course. But she's my sister.

— What did she say?

— Nothing much, she said they'd made it up.

— That's all?

— She said it meant everything to her to know she could rely on us.

— That's good.

— When is she going to grow up? Dorothy says. I'm sick of being her mother. I hate the mess she's got herself into.

— It isn't a mess, he says, looking round to see if there are any other saucepans to wash. It's their life.

— I'm old-fashioned enough to think that people are responsible for their lives, she says.

— You have high standards, he says.

— I believe in the dignity of the human race, she says.

— That's what I mean, he says, not everyone can live up to your ideals.

— I'm not blaming her, she says. Not in any way. And don't get me wrong. I'm not blaming him either, I'd probably act like him myself if I was in his shoes.

— Oh come, he says, rinsing out the sink.

— I mean, she says, I realise how fortunate we are to have found each other. When I look round at our friends I don't see many couples in our situation. But then we've worked for it. We wouldn't settle for less. We are aware of the sanctity of life and of how little it takes to destroy that, and we have made sure it remains that way.

— She's not unhappy, you know, he says. And neither is he. He takes the dischcloth and starts to polish the sink.

— Oh, she says, unhappiness! Half the misery of this world is caused not by men and women being unwilling to stay in their rooms, as Pascal thought, but by the crazy modern belief that we are all entitled to happiness in our lives. That is the curse of our time, she says, dreamed up in the eighteenth century and exported to the world in the twentieth by the USA. Who before Rousseau ever thought we were put on earth to be happy? And, ironically, as a result people were much happier then than they are now. Because they are all desperately searching for happiness, believing it's just round the corner, embodied in a new job, a new lover, perhaps even a new car or a new pair of shoes. And then they find that it isn't, and when the job and the lover and the car and the shoes leave them feeling just as they were before they don't know where to turn, they eat out their hearts and their liver in bitterness till another new job, new lover, new car or new whatever swims into their ken. The triumph of hope over experience, which is how Johnson described a second marriage, she says, is a modern phenomenon, and in picking it out for comment Johnson was showing once again what a spokesman he was for an older notion of ethics, one that goes all the way back to Aristotle, one where experience and hope are not locked in perpetual warfare but form the woof and warp of the one life. Do you know what she told me? she says. She told me that for all their differences she and Charlie were locked together like two escaped prisoners on board a raft that is rapidly approaching a waterfall. Can you imagine such an image ever being used before the Romantic era? Can you envisage a more pessimistic interpretation of life? Life ought to be a gift, not a curse. How come I have a sister who not only thinks but lives the opposite?

— They're quite happy, you know, he says again. I wouldn't say they were unhappy people.

— You think they're playing at being accursed?

— I wouldn't say that. I don't know quite what I think, but it strikes me that neither of them is actually unhappy. In fact I'd say they were a lot happier than most people I know.

— Because they're frivolous?

— No, they're not frivolous. I don't know what it is. They seem to drift along quite well, I'd say.

— If drifting is what you're after, she says.

— It's not what I'm after, he says. And it certainly isn't what you're after. But it suits some people and it seems to suit them.

— Why does she keep trying to leave him all the time then?

— I don't think she does, he says. I think they have their ups and downs like all couples, and like most couples they've devised a strategy for coping that seems to work.

— I don't think a life of ups and downs is a good life, she says. And I wish their strategy for coping didn't always involve us.

He steps back from the sink and observes his handiwork.

— There, he says. I think it's done.

— You want to go to bed?

— I'm knackered.

— You go, she says. I think I'll stay up and read a little. Do you mind?

— I'm too tired to mind, he says.

III

Beatrice puts down the phone and says: — There.

— What did she say?

— What do you think?

— Was she frosty?

— Yes.

They sit awkwardly at the table, the bottle between them.

— I don't know what I was thinking of, she says.

— It's perfectly natural, Charlie says.

— Do you think so?

— I was crazy, he says.

— Were you?

— Irresponsible.

— I suppose you were, she says.

— It's...

— What?

— She's...

— I told you, she says. I don't want to hear about her.

— I'm sorry, he says.

— No, she says, I'm sorry. I know it's irrational of me, but as long as I don't know I...

— Of course, he says. But I wouldn't ever leave you. You know that.

— You can leave me, she says. If that's what you want.

— I told you, he says. It's not what I want.

— Then you have to give her up.

— I told you. I have already.

He shares out the last of the wine and gets up to fetch another bottle.

— I would never give you up, he says. Or the children.

— But I'd leave you, she says. We'd leave you. If you go on seeing her.

— I know, he says.

— But you still go on doing it.

— You don't understand, he says. She threatened to kill herself. She's not stable.

— You shouldn't take up with unstable people.

— Of course I shouldn't.

— Then why do you keep doing it?

— I don't know, he says.

— Yes you do, she says.

— What do you mean?

She cradles the glass with both hands and looks down into it.

— What do you mean? he asks again,

— You know what I mean, she says.

— What?

— I bore you. The family bores you. You want adventure.

— I do?

— I don't mind, she says. But I'm warning you: If it happens again it's all over between us.

— I promised you, he says.

— You promised me before.

He is silent.

— I don't care, she says. It's up to you.

— That's the trouble, he says. You don't care.

He drains his glass and helps himself to more from the newly opened bottle.

— Isn't that a bit unfair? she asks.

— I don't feel any compassion in you, he says, I never have.

— You mean clinging sentimentality and threats of suicide? she asks.

— Don't make fun of her, he says. She suffers.

— And I don't?

— I didn't say that.

— What did you say?

— I said that you've always been like that — not caring.

— Meaning what?

— Meaning that I don't seem to matter to you.

— You don't think you've driven me to it?

— No, he says. I think that's your character.

— Then why do you stay with me?

— I couldn't live without you, he says. Or the children.

— But you don't mind hurting us.

— Of course I do.

— Then why do you do it?

He is silent, sipping his wine.

— I know what you're thinking, she says. You're thinking you do it because I don't care. Because I've never given you the warmth you crave. And perhaps you're right. Perhaps I was always a cold fish.

— You're not a cold fish, he says. You just try to protect

yourself by not caring too much. Perhaps it goes back to your childhood and the love and admiration you felt your parents lavished on your sister and withheld from you.

— Not caring at all or not caring too much? she asks.

— What does it matter?

— It matters a lot, she says.

— I don't know, he says.

— You knew that's how I was from the start, she says. I never tried to hide it.

— No, he says. You never tried to hide it. I liked that in you, as a matter of fact. I found it refreshing to be so unsentimental.

— And what made you change your mind?

— I haven't changed my mind, he says.

— But now I seem cold to you.

— Not cold, he says. Distant.

— It's you who put the distance between us, she says.

— No it isn't, he says. I wanted to be close to you. When the children came I thought I was. We were.

— And now?

— I've just told you.

— Distant.

— Not withdrawn. But as if it no longer mattered.

— It doesn't, she says. You don't believe me but it really doesn't. If you want to go to your Angie you're welcome to her. But not to both of us.

— Why didn't you feel like that about... the others?

— How do you know I didn't?

— You didn't say this kind of thing.

— Perhaps it's just the last straw. Or perhaps it's something about her.

— That she wants me all to herself?

— I told you I didn't want to talk about her.

— But I want to understand.

— You never understand.

— Why do you say that?

— Because it's true.

— Yes, but why now?

— Because it's true now.

They are silent at the kitchen table, the bottle of wine open between them.

— It's true, he says. She frightens me in a way none of the others did. They seemed to know the rules. I don't feel she does.

— It's perfectly understandable, she says. She wants you all to herself. Not bits and pieces of you when you can get away from us.

— I suppose so, he says.

— I've told you, she says. If that's what you want, fine.

— It's not fine, he says, and it's not what I want.

— I don't mind, she says. But you really do have to understand that it's me or her. You can't have both.

— I've never known you so absolute, he says.

— Just make up your mind, she says.

— I told you, he says. It was made up a long time ago.

— Yes, she says, the last time this came up.

— I was worried she'd do something to herself.

— You'll be worried again.

He is silent,

— I don't mind, she says. I told you, I don't mind. But you have to understand that this is the last time.

— I understand, he says,

— I'm not threatening you, she says, I just can't stand it any more.

164

— I understand, he says.

He refills their glasses.

— I understand, he says again.

— I wonder if you do, she says.

— It's so difficult to get free of her, he says.

— That's your problem, she says.

— Of course it's my problem, he says. I just want you to show a little empathy.

— Why should I show empathy? she says. It's your problem.

— You know I love you, he says.

— You have a funny way of showing it, she says.

— I couldn't go on living without you and the children.

— You may have to, she says.

— What do you mean by that?

— If you start again with her.

— No, he says. I've learned my lesson,

— You said that the last time, she says.

— She was going to kill herself, he says.

— She was going to kill herself again, she corrects him.

— All right. All right.

He pours himself some more wine. — Let her, he says. I've done all I could.

— You said that the last time, she says.

— Don't go on about it, he says.

— I just want to make sure you understand.

— I understand.

He is silent, looking down at his glass.

— It's late, she says. We ought to go to bed.

— Yes, he says.

She gets up and he follows, depositing his glass on the sink beside hers.

In bed she says: — It's so demeaning, all this.

He takes her hand. — I'm sorry, he says.

— I don't think you are, she says.

— Why do you throw everything back in my face? he says, suddenly angry.

She is silent.

— It's always the same, he says. I try to move towards you and you just push me away.

— Charlie, she says. You never listen, do you? You want to be a little boy all your life. You want to do all the things you want and then have mummy forgive you. But I'm not your mother. I can't forgive you. You don't seem to live in the same world as anyone else. You feel everyone has to abide by the rules except you. Don't you see yourself? Don't you see how you are? Even now I don't know whether to believe you or not. You probably don't know whether to believe yourself or not. It's twelve years we've been married, she says, and it's been the same story every single year, the same boring story, year after year. I don't know why you didn't leave me ages ago. I don't know why I didn't leave you. Or at least I do know, part of you is a very lovable man and once upon a time I loved you very much. But love is like a fabric that starts to wear thin and finally it tears and all you've got is this torn piece of cloth. You just don't accept your responsibilities, she says. You think if I don't know about things they don't really exist. Well they do, whether I know about them or not, and most of the time I do, of course, because you're not very good at hiding things either. Or perhaps you can't even be bothered to hide them, perhaps you even want me to know about them and to forgive you. Well I can't forgive you. Perhaps your mother could forgive you but a wife can't. You have to understand that, to really understand it, not just say you understand it but really really understand it. And I'm not sure that you do.

He is crying silently now beside her in the dark and stroking her hand, which is still clasped in his. He turns towards her and begins to stroke her breasts and then her stomach and moves his hand lower and strokes her thighs and moves his hand between her thighs as she draws in her breath quickly. He is crying openly now as he rolls on top of her and slides into her, holding her shoulders and saying: I'm sorry I'm sorry I'm sorry I'm sorry.

Afterwards they lie side by side, staring up into the darkness.

She touches his face and feels the wetness. She licks her fingers and tastes the salt.

— I love you, she says.

But he is already asleep.

IV

— Is that Deirdre?

— Who else could it be, Dorothy?

— Your voice sounded funny.

— It always sounds funny on the telephone. I've been meaning to ring and thank you for the other evening. I'm sorry about Alfonso.

— Why sorry?

— He made a bit of a fool of himself, didn't he, with all that business? I'm afraid he's beginning to lose it after a glass or two.

— I thought he was just the same as he always is.

— Did you?

— Listen, Deirdre, Dorothy says, something rather odd has happened.

— Odd?

— Yes. Tony's disappeared.

— Disappeared?

— Yes.

— What do you mean, disappeared?

— He left a note saying he'd be gone for a while and not to

worry about him and I haven't heard a word from him since.

— When was that?

— Yesterday.

— Have you been to the police?

— Well, no, not with that note and everything.

— Is he involved in undercover work?

— Undercover work? What on earth do you mean, Deirdre? Tony's a banker.

— I don't know, Dorothy. There's such an aura about Tony.

— Is there?

— Of course there is. I've often wondered if he was an agent.

— I don't know what you're talking about, Dorothy says. Tony's never been able to keep a secret to save his life.

— It could be his cover, couldn't it? Deirdre says.

— Do you think something's happened to him? Dorothy asks.

— I'm sure there's an explanation, Deirdre says.

— I'll read you his note, Dorothy says. May not be back for a few days. Don't worry. Tony. What on earth does it mean, Deirdre?

— It means you mustn't worry, darling. It'll all get cleared up soon. Perhaps he has a surprise for you.

— What sort of a surprise?

— I don't know. Some sort of surprise.

— It's not really like Tony, she says. It's not the sort of thing he goes in for.

— What about his handwriting?

— What about it?

— Does it show signs of anxiety?

— I don't know. It just looks like his handwriting.

— That's good then. If it showed signs of anxiety it might suggest that he was being pursued. Blackmailed perhaps. Who knows? Or that he had an incurable disease. Or was afraid he was starting to lose his mind.

— How am I supposed to tell if it shows signs of anxiety? Dorothy says.

— Look at the loops, Deirdre says. The loops on the l's.

— There aren't any l's, Dorothy says. But anyway he discusses everything with me. Everything that worries him. He'd have come to me first if it was any of those things.

— Perhaps he couldn't, Deirdre says. Perhaps he'd been told something terrible would happen if he did.

— He still would have, Dorothy says. You know how close we are.

Deirdre is silent

— I found it in the hall, Dorothy says. He must have left it on his way out.

— Has he been acting at all strangely these last few days?

— Of course not. I'd have said.

— It didn't look as if he had anything on his mind?

— Tony always has things on his mind, Dorothy says. You know how he worries about things.

— I'm sure it'll sort itself out, Deirdre says.

— It's just so odd, Dorothy says. It's so out of character.

— I'm sure there's an explanation, Deirdre says.

— Of course there's an explanation, Dorothy says. But it's so odd. I don't know what to think.

— Perhaps you should contact the police, Deirdre says. Perhaps he's lost his mind and you need to inform them so they can alert hospitals and police stations and things.

— But would he have written me that note if he'd lost his mind?

— Perhaps he felt he was losing it and it was the last thing he did before he lost it.

— You know, Deirdre, Dorothy says, sometimes you say the stupidest things.

— I'm just exploring the possibilities, Deirdre says. It's important to explore all the possibilities.

— I don't think that's a possibility, Dorothy says.

— In that case we cross it off, Deirdre says tartly.

— Though I do think the likeliest thing is he's worried about something and needs to think it through on his own, Dorothy says.

— You don't think he's been gambling the bank's money, do you? Nick Leeson sort of thing?

— Tony?

— Well, we live in such strange times, Dot.

— Tony's the soul of probity, Dorothy says.

— Yes, Deirdre says. I expect he is.

— You may be right, Dorothy says. Perhaps he's been for a checkup and his heart's not absolutely one hundred per cent and he needs to think out the implications. Though he would always talk these things over with me. May not be back for a few days. Don't worry. Tony. How on earth am I supposed not to worry?

— It's just to make sure you don't think he's been run over or anything, Deirdre says.

— May not, Dorothy says. That means he's not sure. There's something funny about all this. Something I can't quite put my finger on.

— What you should do, Deirdre says, is take it at its face value. He may be gone for a few days but you're not to worry.

— Why couldn't he tell me?

— Perhaps he didn't want to worry you.

— And you think this worries me less?

— Perhaps he had sworn not to tell anyone.

— We've always told each other everything, Dorothy says. Our marriage is built on absolute openness.

— But you wouldn't want him to break his promise, would you?

— He wouldn't make a promise like that.

— Perhaps he had to. For you. For Sam.

— Do you think he's been taken hostage?

— It's a possibility.

— But then how could he have left that note?

— Perhaps he went voluntarily.

— Why would he have gone voluntarily?

— Perhaps he did it to save you. And Sam.

— I wish you wouldn't keep bringing Sam into it.

— We have to look at every angle, Deirdre says.

— But then he wouldn't say he'd be back in a few days, would he? And besides, nobody's approached me for ransom money or anything like that.

— That's true, Deirdre says. I think, she says, that you'll just have to do what he says and not worry, Dot. He'll turn up in a day or two and everything will be clear.

— I suppose so, Dorothy says.

— Do you want me to come over?

— No no. I can manage.

— I'll ring tomorrow, she says. But let me know if he turns up, will you?

— Of course.

— And — Dot — don't worry. I'm sure there's a perfectly simple explanation.

— I hope so, Dorothy says.

— 'Bye, then.

— 'Bye.

V

Charlie wonders, as he so often does when he sees her, why a woman who in all probability will never see forty again should wear her hair in a fringe, but as always the slight perversity of it, the evident mismatch between the childish fringe and the heavily made-up face beneath makes his loins tingle and his heart beat faster.

— If I cannot see you I will kill myself, Angie says.

— There's no question of not seeing me, Charlie says. Only we've got to be careful for a while.

— I don't want to be careful, Angie says. I want to be able to see you whenever I want. I don't want to have to hide and pretend and snatch an hour or two with you whenever you feel she isn't looking.

— I know, darling, Charlie says. I want that too, just as much as you. But we've got to be patient.

— The time for patience is over, Angie says. The time for acting has arrived.

— I love your absoluteness, Charlie says, and he does, though it frightens him too.

— Love, love, Angie says, with a shake of the head which makes the light gleam on her glossy black hair.

He reaches out across the table and strokes her bare shoulder.

— I mean it, Angie says.

— I know, Charlie says unhappily.

— Then tell her.

— I can't, he says.

— Why not?

— We've been into it, he says. What about the children?

— I thought you'd accepted that a price had to be paid.

— I have, he says.

He strokes her shoulder. — I can't give up the children, Angie, he says. You know that.

— Who talks about giving up? she says. One would think we were in the nineteenth century.

He sits, silent.

— They will only admire you for it, she says.

— Admire me?

— How do they think of you now? she asks.

— Think of me? I don't know.

— I think they feel you are a weakling, she says. But if you take a stand they will respect you.

— I suppose so, he says.

— No doubt, she says.

— I think, though, he says, we should just be a bit careful. While I try to sort things out.

— What do you mean, sort things out?

— I mean it would be easier — like with an appendix, you know? It's always dangerous to take it out when it's inflamed and very dangerous when it's burst. People can die.

— And so?

— Well, it's a bit like that. If we do things while she's inflamed it's... Whereas when things have cooled a bit...

— You're talking rubbish, she says.

— You've got to see it from my point of view, he says.

— I have seen it from your point of view, she says. I've seen it from your point of view for three years. I want to see it from my point of view for a change. I want *you* to see it from my point of view. I want Beatrice to see it from my point of view.

— I know, I know, he says. I talked to her.

— You talked to her?

— I explained the position.

— And?

— She's thinking it over.

— Thinking it over? In the name of God what does she have to think over?

— She's thinking over her response. She asked me to give her a bit of time.

— She asked you that?

— Yes. She begged me to give her a bit of time. I couldn't refuse.

He strokes her shoulder again. — Could I? he says.

— Why didn't you say this from the beginning?

— I tried to. But you wouldn't listen.

She is silent, turning over what he has said.

He strokes her shoulder.

Absentmindedly she takes his hand and puts his little finger in her mouth.

Later, she says: — I've been sick, you know. I had a scare.

— A scare? What kind of scare?

— I felt a lump on my breast.

— You felt what?

— I went to the hospital. They did scans.

She is silent, lying beside him in the dark.

— Feel, she says. Here.

— I can't feel anything.

— Here.

— Yes, he says, withdrawing his hand. What happened?

She is silent.

— Why didn't you tell me?

— How? she says. Call you? And if she's with you when the phone rings?

He is silent.

— You see what I mean? she says.

— I'm sorry, he says. What happened?

— It was negative. They're going to monitor me but they thought it was negative.

— They thought or they knew?

— What does anyone know? she says. They're guessing, half the time.

— But things like that...

— They're guessing, she says.

He is silent.

— And then my supervisor decided I had to submit in the next six months.

— And?

— And what?

— Isn't that possible?

— Charlie, she says. You dear man. Do you never listen to what I say?

— Why do you say that?

— Why do I say that? Because I've told you often enough I'm going to need several years at least. It's not as if I don't have a job, is it? And when I get home in the evening after a day in the shop I can tell you I don't feel like thinking about Poussin. And I don't want to hand in some rotten half-thought-through little piece of work just to satisfy their pathetic requirements. I'm thirty-six years old, Charlie, and I think I'm entitled to work for myself and not simply to fulfil the requirements of the glorious University of London. I told him I would hand it in when it was ready, no sooner and no later.

— What did he say?

She laughs. — They're frightened of me, she says. All of them. All those academics. They've never met anyone like me. So he said it might be difficult and they had to make sure students blah blah blah and I smiled at him and then he shut up.

— Charlie, she says, after a while. Get me a drink will you? There's some white in the fridge. And then if you're a good boy I'll suck your cock.

VI

Dorothy shifts in her seat and gazes about her. The room is uniformly grey and impersonal, as is the man behind the desk. The windows need cleaning, both inside and out. Or perhaps they are made like that to prevent people looking in, or out.

The man behind the desk clears his throat. — You were saying...? he says.

— I'm sorry, Dorothy says. I was momentarily distracted.

The man picks up a gold pencil and begins to doodle on the blank sheet of paper in front of him.

— It's very difficult, Dorothy says. I've never been in this sort of position before.

The man smiles at her without opening his mouth. — Everything we undertake is entirely confidential, he says.

— Of course, Dorothy says.

The man puts his head to one side as though trying to lay it on his shoulder, and looks at her. He waits.

Dorothy is about to speak when he says: — Take your time. Please. Take as much time as you want.

Disconcerted by his words, she finds herself once more unable to speak.

The man waits, doodling on his sheet of paper.

– It's like this, Dorothy says finally. My husband has disappeared.

The man does not appear to have heard. She presses on: – Five days ago I found a note from him in the hall. It said: May not be back for a few days. Don't worry. Tony.

She reaches in her bag and hands him the note. He smoothes it out on top of the sheet of paper on which he has been doodling and examines it.

– May not be back for a few days. Don't worry. Tony, she repeats.

The man reaches in his desk drawer, pulls out an oblong magnifying glass and examines the note with care. Dorothy waits.

The man straightens up and looks at her. – His name is Tony? he asks.

– Yes of course, she says. That's what it says. Don't worry. Tony.

The man bends over the note again.

She waits.

Finally he straightens again, puts the note on one side of the desk and looks at her. – Go on, he says.

– On? she asks.

He nods.

– Of course I worried, she says. This had never happened before. We always tell each other everything. We have a completely open relationship. I wondered whether to go to the police. But I decided not to.

– Very wise, the man says.

– Why?

The man shrugs, raising his eyebrows a little and letting a smile play across his lips, as though to say that it was self-evident.

– I thought I would wait, she says.

The man nods. He places his elbows on the arms of his chair and presses the palms of his hands against each other, the middle fingers just touching the base of his nose, the index fingers just below his lower lip.

– And then today I received this through the post, she says.

She fishes in her bag again and finds a letter in its envelope. She hands it to him.

He leans across the desk and takes it, draws out the letter, spreads it on the sheet of paper in front of him and reads it.

– All well, she says. Don't worry. Back soon. Tony.

The man does not appear to have heard. He reaches once more into his desk drawer, once more emerges with the oblong magnifying glass. He bends over the letter.

Finally he straightens and looks at her over the magnifying glass. – The same hand, he says.

– Of course it's the same hand, Dorothy says. It's Tony's.

The man smiles his fleeting smile and nods his head a little, as though to say one might expect as much from an amateur.

He sighs and puts the magnifying glass back in its drawer, folds the letter and replaces it in its envelope. He places the envelope on one side, next to the note.

– I want you to find him, she says.

The man sighs deeply, as though some long-awaited relief had come at last. He picks up the letter and places it on the sheet of paper in front of him. He gazes at the envelope.

– Have you tried his office? he asks without looking up.

— He's been in every day, she says.

— Have you tried talking to him at the office?

— Yes. He always seems to be busy.

— I see, the man says.

He looks up from the envelope and gazes into her eyes. — You did not try to go in person to the office?

— No.

— I see. He nods thoughtfully, pursing his lips. If I take on this case, he says, I will need to have your full co-operation.

— Of course, Dorothy says.

— Have you read our terms and conditions?

— Your secretary gave them to me in the waiting-room, she says.

— You have read them?

— I was kept waiting long enough to read them.

The man smiles his fleeting smile. — We feel it is better if our clients are fully aware of what we can and cannot offer before the first interview, he says.

— I see.

— You are happy with the terms and conditions?

— I want you to find my husband, she says. I don't want him to know I'm looking for him. I want you to report back to me.

— I understand, the man says.

— How much will it cost?

— How can I say at this stage? the man says.

— Of course, she says. I quite understand. But if it is all fairly simple are we talking in terms of hundreds or of thousands? I may not be able to afford you.

— Let us say hundreds, the man says. Provided there are no complications.

— Naturally, she says.

— If there are, I get back to you and ask you if you wish to proceed, he says. It's like bringing a car to be serviced. The garage will inform you of any unexpected problems and only put them right after you have agreed to the extra cost.

— I understand.

— If you wish me to handle this case — and all our work here is handled personally and confidentially, I need hardly add — if you wish me to handle this case I will have to ask you to sign this agreement and then to provide me with all the information I require.

— What kind of information? she asks, taking the sheet of printed paper he has handed her across the desk.

— The usual things, he says. A recent photo. His office address.

She puts the printed sheet down on her side of the desk and reaches into her bag again. She hands him a photograph. He lays it down on the sheet of paper in front of him and examines it, this time without the magnifying glass.

She quickly reads the printed sheet, takes a pen out of her bag and signs it. She hands it back.

— What do you think of him? she asks.

— Of the photo?

— Yes.

— It's adequate.

— I mean of the man in the photo.

— It's adequate, he repeats.

He puts down the photograph and picks up the printed sheet she has returned to him. He reads it carefully, ticking the occasional passage with his gold pencil.

— How do you propose to pay? he asks.

— How?

— By credit card? By cheque?

— I'd rather pay by cheque.

— Good. As you see, we require a deposit, for obvious reasons. Can you make it out to the above?

He passes the printed sheet back to her.

She takes her cheque book out of her bag and writes out the cheque. She hands it to him.

He examines it, then lays it on his desk beside the photograph, the letter and the note.

— Good, he says, smiling at her.

He gets up, comes round to her side of the desk, holding out his hand. She gets up in turn and, since she does not give him her hand, he takes her elbow and escorts her to the door.

— Have no fear, he says. You will have your information in no time at all.

— I don't want him to know, she says. He would be deeply offended. We have always been open with each other. That is the basis of our marriage.

— Of course, he says. You need have no fear. At Buttons we are all professionals. He will never know a thing.

VII

If it had been hard going up those three flights of stairs it is even harder coming down. Dorothy finds that she is having difficulty breathing. Out in the street once more she tries to gather herself but has to lean against the wall of the building for support.

Across the busy road a Caffè Nero beckons. She waits at the lights and crosses with the crowds. Inside it is suddenly cool and dark. She queues up for her coffee, pays, and looks round for a place to sit. She finds a table by the window and slides into a seat. Carefully she opens her packet of sugar and drops the contents into her cup.

– Dot!

She looks up at the man sitting opposite her,

Seeing her look of bewilderment he says: – Charlie.

– Charlie!

– I thought it was you.

– What are you doing here?

– I was visiting a friend.

– I see.

— And you?

— I had something to do round here.

He stares at her. — It's good to see you, he says.

— And you.

She stirs and sips her coffee. Then becomes aware of his gaze: — What's the matter?

— Nothing. Why?

— You were staring at me.

— Was I?

— Is my hair funny?

— Funny?

— Oh come on! she says.

— I'm sorry. You looked... white.

— I've been having a tough time.

— Oh?

— How's Bea?

— Fine. Fine. We almost split up, as you know.

— Yes.

— Then she changed her mind.

— Yes.

— I couldn't live without her, he says. Or the children. You know that.

— Of course.

— She knows it too.

He is silent, fiddling with his spoon.

— Things are still difficult between us, he says.

— They always have been, she says, laughing suddenly, regaining her composure.

— Have they?

— Well, haven't they?

— Is that what she's told you?

– She doesn't confide in me. You know that.

– She feels you're always judging her.

– I am.

– She feels she can't live up to your high moral standards.

– She can't.

– Still so absolute?

– How can one change, Charlie? At our time of life?

– That's what keeps us together, he says. We know neither of us can change. Not really.

– Bea was always wanting to change, she says. That's the first thing I remember about her. From a tomboy to a girlie girl, from a girlie girl to a bluestocking, from a bluestocking to a good time girl, from a good time girl to I don't know what.

– That's what I mean, he says. She realises now that that's her character. She can't change that.

– Can't change always wanting to change.

He laughs. – You're teasing, he says.

– No. I'm serious.

– And Tony?

– What about him?

– How is he?

– Fine. Fine.

– Give him my regards, will you.

– Of course. You must both come round one of these days.

– Thank you.

He lights a cigarette.

– Give me one, Charlie, she says.

– I thought you'd given up?

– I need one now.

He lights it for her and she inhales and then exhales slowly, with pleasure. – It may be bad for one, she says, but it really is one of the great pleasures of life.

He shrugs.

— You know, she says, you look more French every time I see you.

— So you used to say.

— It's still true.

— Seedier.

— Yes, but in a very French way.

Suddenly she stubs out her cigarette. — I have to go, she says.

— Already?

— Yes.

She stands up. He too stands, on the other side of the low table.

— Dot, he says. Can I say this? *You* look more beautiful every time I see you.

— Thank you, she says.

— You don't mind my saying that?

— Why should I mind?

— I don't know.

— Goodbye, she says.

He leans across the table and kisses her.

— 'Bye, Dot, he says.

VIII

When Beatrice enters the lift in Russell Square tube station she always tries to make for a wall. Usually that is impossible as there are already too many people assembled in the metal box, and she resigns herself to standing squashed, eyes closed, out in the middle.

She is standing thus, lost in her own thoughts, when she feels a hand on her arm. She shifts position without opening her eyes, but the pressure on her arm remains. Angrily she opens her eyes and finds herself looking into a familiar face.

– Alfonso! she exclaims.

There is too much of a crush for conversation to be either possible or desirable, so they wait, smiling at each other, till the lift stops and the doors open.

– Where are you going? he asks.

– Knightsbridge.

– That's my direction.

– Still working for Professor Pennington? he asks as they make their way to the platform and stand, waiting for the train.

– Uhuh.

— I thought I might see you the other day, you know, he says.

— Oh?

— We were having dinner with Tony and Dorothy when you rang.

— She told you I rang?

— Of course.

— It was a dinner party?

— Just a few people.

— And she told you all?

— Uhuh.

— Bitch.

— She just said you were coming over.

— She didn't explain the reason?

— No.

— I see.

— But you didn't come.

— No. I changed my mind.

— Why?

— It's too complicated to go into.

— How's Charlie?

— Fine. Actually I was coming over because I had planned to leave him.

— You had?

— I couldn't take it any longer, Alfonso.

— Couldn't take what?

— The lies. The deceit. The womanising.

— But that's Charlie.

— I know.

— You knew when you accepted him.

— He promised to reform.

The train arrives and they find a seat.

– What stopped you from coming over then?

– He promised to reform.

He looks at her and they both burst out laughing at the same time.

– It's not as simple as that, she says.

– It's never simple, he says.

– He begged me to stay, she says.

– Of course, he says.

– He said he would be lost without us.

– Of course, he says again,

– I don't know why I believed him, she says.

– You didn't, he says. You only wanted to hear him say it.

– Is that it?

– Uhuh.

– Why?

– One needs these things.

– Even if one doesn't believe them?

– Even if one doesn't believe them.

She is silent, digesting this.

Finally she says: – It's good to see you, Alfonso.

– And you.

– How's life treating you?

– Oh, you know, Beatrice, one carries on.

– And Deirdre?

– She's good. She gave up the job.

– She gave it up? But you had all those perks. All those restaurants to go to.

– She got fed up having always to evaluate what she was eating. It did things to her digestion, you know what I mean? Now she writes her books and travels the world adjudicating competitions.

— Not bad.

— They put her up in a nice hotel and often there are messages to her from strangers saying they've heard she's in town and their grandmothers used to make them such a delicious so and so and they still have the recipe and would she like to come over if she's free one evening and taste it what an honour it would be and so on.

— It sounds like a great life. You go with her?

— Sometimes. Most of the time I prefer to stay here. Besides, she likes to travel alone.

— She does?

— It means she can pick up young men whenever she feels like it.

— No!

— No, he says. At least I don't think so.

— For a moment I thought you were serious.

— Deirdre likes food and she likes her comfort, he says. I think she quite likes me. I'm not sure she likes sex.

— I never know when you're having me on, Alfonso.

He smiles, pleased, and strokes his beard.

— I suppose she doesn't put on any weight, she says.

— No, she's as slim as a teenager.

— The bitch.

— Even I envy her, he says.

— You're pretty slim too, Alfonso.

— I'm afraid not, he says. Clothes hide a great deal, you know.

— Here's my stop, she says.

— I'll call you one of these days, he says. I get lonely when Deirdre's away.

— Do that, she says. It would be good to see you, Alfonso.

IX

— I have photographs, Dorothy says on the phone. There's no possibility of doubt.

— What do you mean you have photographs? Deirdre says. How could you have photographs?

— I hired a detective, Dorothy says. He took the photographs.

— You shouldn't have done that, Deirdre says.

— I was at my wits' end, Dorothy says. I was sick with worry. I never imagined it would turn out to be this kind of utter banality.

— There may be an explanation, Deirdre says. You should wait till you hear his side of the story.

— He hasn't come home. It looks as if he has no intention of coming home. But there it is in black and white.

— It's never black and white, Deirdre says.

— It is here, Dorothy says. Though the photographs are in colour.

— They're only photographs, Deirdre says. After all.

— What do you mean only photographs? Dorothy says. They show him arm in arm with his secretary. His secretary! Only a man bereft of all sense of style would fail to see that these things simply cannot be allowed to happen.

— I still think there may be an explanation, Deirdre says.

— And it's not even as though she was pretty, Dorothy says. She's dowdy and… what's the word? Unprepossessing.

— Perhaps only to you, Deirdre says.

— No, Dorothy says. Objectively. I'll show you the photos when we meet.

— Photos can lie, Deirdre says.

— These don't, Dorothy says. They tell the truth exactly as it is.

— How do you know?

— I've met the woman, Dorothy says. She's been to my house. I could never in a thousand years imagine Tony would get involved with her.

— You couldn't believe Tony could get involved with anyone, Deirdre says.

— No, Dorothy says. What we had between us was far too precious for that.

— So you see, Deirdre says. There must be another explanation.

— He's living with her in Southend-on-Sea.

— Where?

— Southend-on-Sea.

— How do you know?

— The detective told me.

— It was a mistake to go to a detective, Deirdre says.

— I was beside myself with worry, Dorothy says. Two notes, both of them saying he was fine and not to worry. Isn't that enough to make one worry oneself sick?

— Perhaps it's a film. Deirdre says. Perhaps he's taking part in a film.

— Why should Tony take part in a film?

— Perhaps it was meant to be a surprise, Deirdre says. For your birthday.

— My birthday isn't for ages.

— Well, films take a long time to make.

— Arm in arm with her, Dorothy says. And she's not even pretty. It's so shaming.

— And you've had no word from him?

— I can't believe it, Dorothy says. Not with what there was between us.

— What else did the detective report?

— Everybody has cameras now, Dorothy says. Traffic wardens have cameras. They photograph your windscreen. As proof of violation.

— What has that got to do with it?

— Tiny little things, Dorothy says. Yet they can take the most detailed pictures. She has a trouser suit on. I ask you. It's so... secretarial.

— What else did the detective say?

— He hasn't finished the investigation.

— You must confront him, she says. Call him at the office and get him to talk to you.

— He pretends he's not in.

— Then go round and confront him.

— No, Dorothy says. I'm not going to demean myself like that. I had a tutor at university, she says, who was in the middle of separating from his wife and she would barge into our tutorials with their little boy and the shopping and start to take things out of the shopping bag and throw them at him, screaming the most horrible things as she did so. With me sitting there with my essay half read. I vowed there and then never ever to get myself in her position.

— But you're not in her position, Deirdre says. You merely want to know what's going on.

— I shall wait for him to tell me, she says. And then I shall divorce him.

— Come on, Dot, Deirdre says. We're not there yet.

— Oh yes we are, Dorothy says.

— And Sam?

— He should have thought about Sam before going to live with his secretary in Southend-on-Sea.

— Nobody tells you he's living with his secretary, Deirdre says.

— My detective does.

— And you believe what he says?

— I paid him to find out.

— He's only human, Deirdre says. He could well have made a mistake.

— Do you think he'd still be in business if he made mistakes of that sort?

— I'm just saying, Deirdre says, that he's only human. Mistakes get made. You've got to wait till you know more.

— Photographs don't lie, Dorothy says. I remembered her as dowdy and dowdy she is. With a black trouser suit. The kind charisma specialists tell you to wear if you have an image problem.

— Charisma specialists? Deirdre says. Image problem? What are you talking about?

— I saw a programme about them on the telly, Dorothy says.

You pay them a lot of money to raise your self-esteem and they tell you what to wear.

— Just like psychoanalysts once did, Deirdre says.

— Psychoanalysts never told you what to wear, Dorothy says. They were always notoriously badly dressed.

— I don't mean that, Deirdre says. Dot, she says, do you want to come round and talk about it?

— I haven't slept for three nights, Dorothy says. I can't believe what I'm living through.

Deirdre is silent.

— It's a bad joke, Dorothy says. Living with his secretary in Southend-on-Sea.

— What was the detective's assessment?

— I didn't pay him to make assessments, Dorothy says. I paid him to find out the facts.

Deirdre is silent.

— Are you still there? Dorothy asks after a time.

— Yes, Deirdre says.

— He'll have to come home at some point, Dorothy says. All his things are here.

— Perhaps he's frightened to come home, Deirdre says.

— Frightened?

— Perhaps he's afraid to face you.

— He knows I would act reasonably, Dorothy says. I'm not going to make a row. That's not my style.

— Perhaps he would rather have a row, Dot, Deirdre says.

— It's not my style, Dorothy says. If he chooses to go and live with his secretary that's his business. I never tried to hold him. Our relationship was never based on rules and regulations. He knows that.

— I have to go, Deirdre says. Alfonso's waiting for me.

— I'm sorry, Dorothy says. I didn't mean to take up your time.

— Not at all, Deidre says. Look, she says, I'll call you tomorrow. Meanwhile, don't jump to conclusions. Not until you've spoken to Tony. All right?

— The conclusions jump at me, Dorothy says. The conclusions are that he has demeaned himself and me by leaving me without an explanation and going to live with this dowdy woman in a trouser suit in Southend-on-Sea.

— Yes, Deirdre says. That's how it looks at the moment, but let's just see how it pans out, all right?

— I'm sorry to have taken up your time, Dorothy says.

— Don't be silly, Deirdre says. That's what friends are for.

— Hand in hand, Dorothy says. With the sea in the background. It beggars belief.

— Goodbye, darling, Deidre says.

— It beggars belief, Dorothy says.

X

When the train stops at Covent Garden and the doors open a man gets into the carriage carrying several laden shopping bags. With a shock Beatrice realises that it is her brother-in-law.

— Tony! she says.

He sits down on the empty seat next to her and kisses her on the cheek.

— What are you up to?

— Been doing a bit of shopping.

— Aren't you going in the wrong direction?

— Aren't you?

— I'm meeting someone.

— So am I.

— With all that? You look as if you're changing your wardrobe. How's Dorothy?

— We've separated.

— What?

He is silent.

— What did you say?

— I said we'd separated.

— Tony, she says, that's not possible.

— Why not?

— It's not possible.

After a while she says: — What happened?

— Nothing.

— But she's perfect! Beatrice says.

— Uhuh.

She is silent. Then she says: — She never told me.

— You've spoken to her?

— No.

— Well then.

— You're right.

After a while she says: — But what happened? Have you moved out? Where are you living?

— Southend-on-Sea.

— Southend-on-Sea? Why?

— It's somewhere to live.

— You walked out on her?

He is silent.

— And Sam?

— She won't let me see him. We're trying to sort that out.

— So you mean it? You're serious?

He is silent.

— Oh Tony, she says. You were so perfect together.

— You're sweet, he says.

— You were. You were always meant for each other.

— Only you could say that, he says.

— What do you mean?

He is silent.

— Oh! she says, laughing. I see.

He is silent.

— Even then, she says. Even then I could see you were meant for each other.

— As you and Charlie were?

— No no. We simply drifted into it.

— And how do you know we didn't?

— Because you were meant for each other.

He is silent.

— You told me that, she says. But I knew it anyway. Do you remember?

— I was a fool, Bea.

— No you weren't, she says. You're a fool now.

He is silent.

— Talk to her, she says. Make it up.

— It's too late.

— It's never too late.

— It is here.

— It's so sudden, she says. I can't believe it.

He is silent.

— But why Southend-on-Sea? she says.

— I've got a friend there.

— A friend? From work?

— Uhuh.

— And he's putting you up?

— Uhuh.

— What have you told him?

— It's a she.

— A she?

— Uhuh.

— Oh Tony! she says. Why?

He shrugs.

— I don't know what to say, she says. And here's my stop.

— Go on. Get off.

— Oh, Tony. Go back to her.

He is silent.

— You'll have forgotten it in six months, she says.

— It's not like that, he says.

— Oh Tony! she says.

He kisses her. — You're sweet, he says.

She stands on the platform, waving as the doors shut. He smiles through the window and waves back.

XI

— Well, well, Charlie says. Something, I see, keeps bringing you to this part of the world. He gets up and kisses her on the cheek.

— I have an appointment. I'm early, Dorothy says.

— Have a seat.

— I didn't expect to see you here, she says, sitting down opposite him at the window.

— Wasn't it here we last met?

— Yes.

— Well then.

She stirs her coffee.

— Hairdresser? he asks her.

— No. And you?

— Me?

— What brings you here?

— I told you. I have a friend nearby. She lives round the corner.

— Ah yes, she says. Bea told me.

— Bea? You talk to her?

— She was going to come and stay. Don't you remember?

— Oh, that, he says. That was a long time ago.

— Yes, she says. It certainly feels like it.

She sips her coffee.

— Same friend? she asks.

— You know how it is with me and Bea, Charlie says. We lead pretty independent lives. But we need each other. And the children of course.

— Tony's left me, Dorothy says. He's living with his secretary in Southend-on-Sea.

— Say that again? Charlie says.

— Tony's left me. He's living with his secretary in Southend-on-Sea.

He begins to laugh.

— You find it funny? she asks.

— No, he says, I'm sorry. I didn't mean you to say it again. It was just a way of expressing amazement. And then you did. And it was funny. So I laughed.

— It's not funny, she says.

— No, he says. I appreciate that.

She sips her coffee.

— When did this happen? he asks.

— A fortnight ago.

— A fortnight ago?

— He left a note in the hall saying not to worry and he'd be back in a day or two and I haven't heard from him since.

— Then how do you know he's living in Southend-on-Sea with his secretary?

— I hired a detective to find out.

— You hired a detective? How did you get hold of one?

— I looked in the Yellow Pages.

— In the Yellow Pages? Had you ever done that sort of thing before?

— Of course not. Nothing like this has ever happened to me before.

— But you went off and hired a detective you found in the Yellow Pages? I didn't even know they advertised in the Yellow Pages.

— I tried to reach him at the office, she says, but though they said he was there, which was a relief in some ways as I was thinking of going to the police, he was never available to talk to me, and though I left messages he never got back to me. So I hired a private detective to find out what was going on and he came back with irrefutable proof that Tony was living in Southend-on-Sea with his secretary.

— What sort of irrefutable proof?

— Photographs. Coloured photographs. Hand in hand with his secretary with the sea in the background.

— How did you know it was the secretary?

— I'd met her. Tony brought her round to dinner. With her dentist husband.

— And the dentist?

— I haven't a clue.

— This is either a bad dream or a silly joke, Charlie says.

— No, Dorothy says. It's the reality.

— But you and Tony were made for each other, Charlie says.

— That's what I thought, Dorothy says. He obviously thought otherwise.

— You don't think there may be a perfectly innocent explanation for it all?

— What kind of explanation would that be?

— I don't know. Perhaps he's making a film. Or engaged in

clandestine anti-terrorist operations.

— It's funny how people's minds run along the same worn tracks, Dorothy says. Deirdre said just the same thing.

— Deirdre Maragal?

— Uhuh.

— Well, perhaps it's because it's the truth.

— Don't be silly, Charlie, Dorothy says.

— I don't think you should jump to conclusions till you've talked to him, Charlie says.

— I'm waiting to do just that, she says. When he finally comes to see his son.

— You've told Sam?

— Of course. We hide nothing from each other.

— About the secretary?

— I showed him the photographs.

— You showed…? You don't think that was unwise?

— Why unwise?

— Well, a child, it might upset him. To see his father hand in hand with a pretty young woman.

— His secretary is blowsy, Charlie, Dorothy says. Blowsy. And hardly young.

— Well, I don't know, hand in hand with someone who isn't you.

— Sam is twelve.

— That's what I mean.

— In earlier generations boys went out to work at twelve.

— What's that got to do with it?

— I hide nothing from him, she says.

— Don't you think perhaps you should?

— Why?

— All right. You probably know best.

— He's my son, she says. And his.

— How's that going to work out?

— How do you mean?

— Well, if you...

— It isn't an issue, Dorothy says. Sam stays with me. Of course I shall make sure he sees his father regularly. On my terms.

She presses the napkin to her lips and looks at her watch.

— Appointment, he says.

— Uhuh.

— The detective! he says. Of course! How silly of me! But why don't you communicate by phone?

— He prefers to hand over the photographs in person.

— More photographs?

— So it seems.

She gets up and he rises with her.

— Dot, he says, taking her hands in his. I'm sorry. If there's anything I can do...?

She smiles at him. — I can handle it, she says. And, besides, you have your own problems.

— Oh, he says, I've learned to live with those.

— Goodbye, Charlie.

— Goodbye, Dot.

He stands, watching her weave between the tables. When she reaches the door he hurries after her. He catches up with her in the street.

— Dot...

She turns, surprised.

— I just thought... Would you like me to wait?

— Wait?

— Just to be here when you come out.

— What for?

— I just thought it might be nice for you to have someone there. You know. In case you felt...

— You're sweet, Charlie. But I can manage on my own. Thank you all the same.

He watches her disappear round the corner.

XII

Bea climbs the stairs of the house in Hans Crescent. She spurns lifts, even when laden with shopping, feeling, rightly, that urban dwellers take too little exercise and should never pass up an opportunity to make this good. She rings the bell of a flat on the fourth floor and then pushes the door open.

— Hullo! she calls.

— I've made some tea, Lionel calls back. I'm on the balcony.

— Do I need a cup?

— I've got two here.

She sits down opposite him and pours herself one.

— Hullo! he says, smiling at her.

She smiles back: — Hullo.

They sit on the narrow balcony, facing each other across the little table.

She sips her tea. — It's still hot, she says.

— I just made it. Have a lemon tart.

— I can't resist your lemon tarts, she says.

— Not mine, he says. A little shop down the road.

— I've just seen my brother-in-law, she says. He's left my sister.

— Gosh! Lionel says.

— I don't understand it.

— She hadn't told you?

— We don't speak much.

— You mean you never speak?

— Hardly ever. I thought of them as a refuge. If anything went wrong. Always there. You know? So it's difficult to take in.

— What did he say?

— He said he'd moved out.

— He didn't say why?

— No.

— He met someone else?

— That's what I don't understand, she says. He's not that kind of person. But he admitted in the end he was living with another woman.

— More tea?

— Thanks.

She holds out her cup.

— It's so untypical, she says.

— Those sorts of things never make any sense, Lionel says.

— I can't understand it, she says.

— It's knocked you up a bit, hasn't it? he says, gazing at her.

— It's just so sudden. I can't think what my sister's going through.

— Where did you meet him?

— In the tube. I keep meeting people I know in the tube. It must be a sign of something.

Lionel takes her hand and strokes it.

— If he'd been five minutes later or had got into another carriage I'd never have known.

— Your sister wouldn't have told you?

— I suppose eventually I'd have heard. He just dropped it in at the end. About this other woman. I thought they'd had a quarrel or something.

— Perhaps it's just a fling.

— Tony doesn't do flings, she says. He takes everything to heart.

— Who is she?

— The other woman?

— Uhuh.

— I don't know. He didn't say. He just said he'd moved in with a friend in Southend-on-Sea and then it came out it was a woman. I can't get over it.

— These things happen, Lionel says, bringing her hand up to his lips and kissing it lightly.

— Not to them it doesn't, she says.

He kisses her hand again. Gently, she withdraws it.

— I suppose it does, she says.

He lets her be.

Finally he says: — One can't hope to understand these things. One just has to accept them.

— That's such a stupid thing to say, she says.

He is silent.

— I'm sorry, he says.

He lets her be.

She looks at her watch: — Shall we...? she says.

— I wasn't sure if you...?

She laughs. — That's what I came for, isn't it?

— I don't know. I thought...

She gets up. He follows her into the bedroom.

He draws the curtains and removes the bedspread, which he folds and lays over a chair.

They each undress in a corner and avert their eyes as they make their way to the bed.

When he turns to her under the sheets and holds her she sighs in the way she always does, more deeply than any other woman he has known. But as he tries to kiss her she pushes him away.

— Let's lie like this a little, she says.

They turn over onto their backs.

— What are you thinking? he asks her.

— Nothing.

— About them?

— No. Nothing.

He is silent.

Finally she says: — Kiss me.

He turns over and leans on his elbows. Her eyes are closed.

— Kiss me, she says again.

He leans over her and brushes her lips with his.

— Thank you, she says. Do it again.

He does it again.

XIII

— Do you have a moment? Dorothy asks.

— Of course, Deirdre says. I fly to Johannesburg this evening, she adds.

— To Johannesburg? Why?

— I'm judging a competition.

— A food competition?

— Uhuh.

— They have that sort of thing in South Africa?

— You'd be surprised.

— You must be busy packing, I'll call when you get back.

— No no. It's good to talk to you. How are things?

— Terrible, Dorothy says.

Deirdre waits.

— We had a talk, Dorothy says.

— He came round?

— Finally, Dorothy says.

— And?

— Nothing.

— What do you mean?

— He's living with his secretary.

— You knew that, Deirdre says.

— You should see her, Dorothy says. So… dumpy. And dresses like a… Terrible.

— You knew all that, Deirdre says. Didn't he give any explanation?

— He said he wasn't up to me.

— Up to you?

— He said I should be married to Pascal.

— Pascal who?

— Pascal. The thinker.

— He said you should be married to him?

— Yes.

— What does he mean?

— How should I know? That's what he said. That he wasn't up to me and I should have been married to Pascal. Or Descartes.

— I see.

— He said he worshipped me but I should have been married to Pascal or Descartes.

— Is he deranged or something?

— I don't know. He said he was frightened of me.

— Frightened of you? Why?

— If you knew what I've sacrificed for that man, Dorothy says.

— You've dedicated your life to him, Deirdre says.

— I told him he would have to see Sam entirely on my terms. I told him I had photos of the two of them, taken by a private detective. In colour.

— What did he say?

— He said he was surprised I stooped to such depths.

— You told him where he could put his depths?

— I did.

— You told him you intended to sue for divorce?

— I did.

— What did he say?

— He said that he hadn't wanted it to be this way but that he couldn't go on. That I was destroying his self-esteem. That I constantly made him feel small and insignificant.

Deirdre is silent.

— I told him I was sure that would not happen with Lola.

— Is that her name?

— Believe it or not, it is.

— She's Spanish?

— No. English. She's called Lola McKenzie.

— That sounds Scottish to me, Dorothy says.

— That's her husband's name, Dorothy says. She's married to a dentist.

— And where is he, the dentist?

— He died of cancer.

— I see, Deirdre says. And what did he say?

— Who?

— Tony. When you said you were sure it wouldn't happen with Lola.

— He said that was exactly it. That Lola made him feel valued. Not judged all the time.

Deirdre is silent.

— Then he started to cry, Dorothy says. And said he had hoped to be able to live up to me, that I had constantly inspired him, that he would always only ever love me and that I was the most beautiful and spiritual and perfect person he had ever known. It was awful. I took it for a while and then I told him to stop it and of course he did.

— Why of course?

— What do you mean why of course?

— You said you asked him to stop it and of course he did.

— Did I?

— Yes.

— I don't know, Dorothy says. I don't know why I said that.

Deirdre is silent but when it is clear that Dorothy is not going to speak she says: — So you're going ahead with the divorce?

— Of course.

— It sounds to me as if he wanted to return, Deirdre says.

— He's broken my heart, Dorothy says. But you know what I'm like. I wouldn't have him back. Not if he begged me.

— Not for Sam's sake?

— He's broken something in me, Dorothy says. By this folly of his. I could never have him back. Not if he begged me.

— That's how you feel at the moment, Deirdre says. You're angry and humiliated. But you've got to think of all there was between you.

— I will never forget that, Dorothy says. Never. And you know I'm not the sort of person to bear grudges. But people have to be responsible for their actions. They can't just do something and then expect everything to be what it was like before they did it. Otherwise life is meaningless.

Deirdre is silent.

— A part of me will never cease to love him, Dorothy says. But I see now that he was always weak and insecure. If I frightened him that's not my fault, she says. Besides, why did he have to lie to me about this woman? Why did he have to say all that about going away for a few days and not to worry?

— He's frightened of you, Dot, Deirdre says. He said so himself.

— Could you live with a man who was frightened of you? Dorothy asks.

Deirdre thinks about this. Finally she says. — No. Thank God that has never arisen between me and Alfonso.

— No, Dorothy says. I suppose not.

— What are you going to do? Deirdre asks.

— I told him, Dorothy says. I will go ahead with the divorce. On my terms.

— On your terms?

— I hold all the cards.

— Nobody holds all the cards these days, Deirdre says.

— It doesn't matter what the courts say, Dorothy says. He will do what I say.

— I'm really sorry, Deirdre says. I liked Tony.

— I loved him, Dorothy says. But he has dug his own grave.

— You two seemed such a perfect couple, Deirdre says. I still think there's been a misunderstanding. Can't you give things a chance to develop?

— You know what I'm like, Dorothy says. And Tony knows what I'm like. I'm absolute. I don't like to fudge things.

— You're sure you won't regret it?

— Regret what? Dorothy says. He may come to regret what he's done, but you know me. I've always lived according to my principles. I can love Tony and despise him at the same time. That's not a contradiction. That's human nature. And I couldn't live with someone I despised, even if he came crawling back begging to be given another chance. Do you understand what I'm saying?

— I understand, Dot, I understand, Deirdre says. I have to go now. I have a plane to catch at six this evening and I haven't even begun to pack.

— It won't last, Dorothy says. One can see that a mile off. But that's what he's opted for and that's what he's getting.

— I'll be back next week, Deirdre says. I'll give you a ring then.

— He knew what I was like, Dorothy says. I don't hold any grudges but the one thing I can't stand is lies and prevarication.

— I know just what you mean, Deirdre says.

— I don't suffer fools gladly, Dorothy says. But I have always given credit where credit is due.

— I know, Deirdre says.

— It's the only way I know how to live, Dorothy says.

— I know, Deirdre says. I'll call you just as soon as I return.

XIV

— Tony's walked out on Dot, Bea says to her husband.

— I know, Charlie says.

— You know?

— I saw Dot. She told me.

— She told you? Where did you see her? Why didn't you tell me?

— I thought it was confidential.

— Confidential? Since when is Dot confiding in you? Where did you see her?

— I was sitting in a café in Kingsway and there she was.

— What were you doing in a café in Kingsway?

— I'd been seeing someone in Covent Garden.

— And Dot was there?

— She came in and sat down at my table. She didn't even recognise me at first.

— And then she told you? Like that?

— How did you hear?

— I saw Tony on the tube. He told me all about it.

— Fancy meeting him on the tube.

— I was looking at this man struggling with all these parcels and then I realised it was Tony.

— What did he have all those parcels for?

— I think he was buying clothes. He's left everything in the house, as far as I could understand.

— He just walked out on her. He's gone off to live with his secretary in Southend-on-Sea.

— I think she drove him to it, Beatrice says.

— You think so? Why?

— I have that feeling.

— Because she's your sister?

— Maybe.

— She was pretty cut up, Charlie says. She couldn't believe it was happening.

— At least it'll stop her lecturing me all the time, Beatrice says.

— That's a pretty hard thing to say, Charlie says.

— Well it's true.

— She's been to see a private detective, Charlie says. Isn't she amazing? Do you know anyone else who's ever employed a private detective?

— No, Beatrice says. But trust her to do it.

— She says she looked in the Yellow Pages, Charlie says. He brought her photos. Tony and this woman, Lola.

— Lola Whitehead? She was at school with me.

— Why should it be Lola Whitehead? There must be thousands of Lolas around.

— Have you ever met one?

— No. But there must be thousands. Anyway, there was Tony hand in hand with this woman with the sea in the background. In colour.

— What do you mean in colour?

– The chap took coloured photos.

– The detective?

– That's what she said.

– She showed them to you?

– No, of course not. She was all upset.

– Especially to be seen by you in that state.

– Why by me?

– She's always despised you.

– You forget we were once engaged.

– No I don't. I'm just repeating what you told me.

– That's true, Charlie says.

– I felt sorry for her, he says after a while.

– I felt sorry for Tony, Beatrice says. He must have been really driven to take a step like that.

– Plenty of men do it without being driven.

– Not Tony. He's an idealist. He'd invested a lot in that marriage.

– You forget that he was once my best friend, Charlie says.

– That's true. I felt sorry for him, though, she says. I don't think he cares much for that Lola. I think she's more of an excuse.

– An excuse for what? Abandoning his wife and child?

– No. Leaving an impossible situation.

– Her hair's turning white, you know, he says.

– Turning white?

– Plenty of white hairs anyway.

– I've got some too.

– I know.

– We're none of us getting any younger.

– But still. Thirty-seven.

– Keats was dead by then.

– What's that got to do with it?

— So was Beethoven.

— You mean Mozart.

— No I mean Beethoven.

— He died much later.

— Later than what?

— Later than thirty-seven.

— Did he? It's all the same thing.

— You talk a lot of rubbish, you know, he says.

— So you often tell me.

— But it doesn't stop you, does it?

— I don't think it's rubbish, that's why.

— Why what?

— Why I don't stop. Now will you please get out of the kitchen so I can tidy up?

— I'll put the things in the machine.

— I thought you could have done that ages ago.

— We were talking.

— Can't you talk and clear up?

— Not if it's a serious conversation.

— And this was serious?

— Never mind, he says, getting up from the table. Never mind.

— No, she says. What do you mean?

— Never mind, he says.

— But I do mind, she says.

— That's too bad.

— Look, she says. Just leave everything, will you? Leave everything and get out. Please. I beg you.

— As you wish, he says stiffly.

— Thank you, she says.

XV

— Hullo? Charlie says. Is that Dot?

— Speaking.

— It's Charlie.

— Charlie! I thought the voice was familiar.

— I haven't been seeing you in the café, Dot. I wondered how you were.

— That's very kind of you, Charlie, she says. But I've finished with all that.

— With the detective?

— Yes.

— Tony's returned?

— Returned? No. Of course not. But I've got enough documentation to go ahead with the divorce. On my terms.

— That's it then, is it?

— What do you mean, that's it?

— No going back?

— There was never any question of that, she says. Not once I understood what had happened. It isn't Tony's view of course.

— Why is that?

— Now he talks of wanting to come back.

— But you don't want him.

— It's not a matter of wanting, Charlie. I can't even if I wanted to. He destroyed the trust between us for ever by his actions. There was never any going back from that.

— I don't know, Charlie says. If you both feel...

— It's not a question of what we feel, Charlie, she says. It's just a fact of life.

— You don't think that for Sam's sake...?

— On the contrary. Sam would never want us to get together again just because we thought it was better for him.

— No, I see that. I just thought...

— Do you know what he said to me?

— Sam?

— No. Tony.

— You've spoken to him?

— Yes. He's been round.

— What did he say?

— He said I should have been married to Pascal.

— Is that a compliment?

— I took it as such.

— Yet you married him.

— I was in love with him. And, besides, he begged me. He said he would kill himself if I didn't.

— He said that?

— Yes.

— Romantic bastard, Charlie says.

— He meant it, Dorothy says.

— Of course, Charlie says.

She is silent,

— But now he thinks Pascal would have been a more suitable partner for you, he says.

— Or Descartes.

— Descartes? He whistles. Was either of them married? he asks.

— No.

— I see.

— But he'd leave this woman if I'd have him back.

— He would?

— Yes. He says she bores him. He says I never bored him.

— But he bored you?

— Why do you say that?

— I just felt it in your voice. And what he said about Pascal.

— He used to be so funny, she says.

— Funny? Tony?

— You didn't think so?

— Unconsciously, you mean?

— No no. He told such good jokes. He still does.

— Oh, Charlie says. Jokes.

— He made me laugh so much, she says. You don't know what it meant to me after the ever-so-serious upbringing I'd had.

— More than me? he asks.

— You?

— He made you laugh more than me?

— Oh, she says, taken aback. You were different,

— I didn't make you laugh?

— Of course you did, but...

— I wasn't as romantic? Is that it?

— Partly, she says.

— And look where it's got you both, he says.

— Nothing's got anyone anywhere, she says. Tony took a decision and I took a decision in the light of that and there we are. It has nothing to do with his romanticism or anything else.

— Maybe, Charlie says.

She is silent.

— Dot, he says, can I come round and see you some time?

— What for?

— I'd like to see you.

— That's kind of you, she says.

— Kind? Why kind?

— I don't know. I thought you wanted to comfort me and I thought it was kind because I'm not much fun at the moment.

— I hadn't worked it out like that, he says. Perhaps you should have been married to Pascal after all. I don't know much about him, I have to confess. I remember we did 'L'homme est un roseau, mais un roseau pensant' at school, but that's about it. And his wager. We did his wager.

— That's what's so stupid about what Tony said, she says. That wager is enough to put anyone off Pascal for ever.

— What was it again?

— Since the chance of there being a God is as great as the chance of there not being a God, and since it doesn't matter what we think or how we act if there isn't but it does if there is, one might as well believe and then there's an even chance we'll get to heaven. Can you imagine founding a life on that?

— It's a bit more complicated than that, isn't it? he says. It's all political, isn't it, and against the Jesuits?

— Oh, she says, you always wanted to argue.

— Not argue, he says. Just get things straight.

— All right. Get things straight.

— So you'd like me to come round and see you?

— If you want to.

— I wouldn't ask if I didn't want to.

— That's true. I always knew where I stood with you, Charlie.

— That's the advantage of not being a romantic, he says.

— I'm busy this week, she says. Give me a ring next week and let's fix something.

— Goodbye, Dot. Viva la joia.

— You always were an idiot, Charlie, she says, laughing.

XVI

— All your friends were shocked, Alfonso says.

— That's not my fault, Tony says.

— I'm not blaming you, Alfonso says, stroking his beard. I wouldn't dream of it. I was merely stating a fact.

— If you knew how small she made me feel, Tony says.

— I don't want to know, Alfonso says.

— How mean.

Alfonso holds up a hand.

— How petty.

— Please, Alfonso says.

— How... unspiritual.

— Perhaps you'd have felt that anyway.

— Perhaps, Tony says drily.

— Which doesn't mean you are any of those things, Alfonso hastens to reassure him.

— Is it a big deal if I am?

— Not at all.

— She made it a big deal, he says.

— I never noticed, Alfonso says.

— You didn't live with her.

— But I've known her a long time.

— It's not the same thing.

— You know me, Alfonso says. I don't pass judgements.

— I know, Tony says. That's why I wanted to talk to you.

— If that's what you had to do that's what you had to do, Alfonso says. End of story.

— I think I made a mistake, Tony says

— You made a mistake? When?

— Not in leaving her, Tony says. But with Lola.

— You made a mistake with Lola? Alfonso says. What kind of a mistake?

— It just seemed the natural thing, Tony says.

— What kind of a mistake?

— I mean, Tony says, I'm so weak I couldn't have done it by myself.

— You needed an excuse.

— Not an excuse. But it would have seemed so wilful just to... you know.

— So you got involved with Lola.

— Well, not exactly. I thought she understood me and...

— She doesn't?

— Well, Tony says, she has her own agenda.

— Her own agenda? Alfonso says with surprise. I don't believe you.

— Are you being sarcastic?

— Me? God forfend!

— It's not funny, Tony says. Not for me, at any rate.

— At least you can see that it might be for other people, Alfonso says. We're making progress.

— I feel miserable all the time, Tony says. I feel I've let Dot down and I feel I'm letting Lola down.

— Why not just worry about yourself? Alfonso says.

Tony is silent.

— Why do you feel you've let Lola down? Alfonso asks.

— I don't feel at ease with her.

— That's understandable, Alfonso says.

— Understandable?

— You used her to get away from Dot, Alfonso says. And now you've got away you look at her and wonder how you're going to get through the rest of your life with her.

— She's very kind, Tony says.

— I'm sure.

— She doesn't make me feel small.

— That's good.

— She's had a hard time. Her husband died of cancer.

— That's terrible.

— I look back and think of those fifteen wasted years with Dot. Of all the humiliation I endured.

— There was Sam, Alfonso says.

— Of course. There was Sam.

— Don't forget Sam.

— No. You're quite right. And she had style. You can't say she didn't have style. That's why I fell in love with her. For her style. Her imperiousness. Her sense that she knew exactly what she wanted out of life.

— You still love that, Alfonso says.

— I still love that, Tony says.

— But you find it humiliating to be with her.

— Yes.

— Yet you're unhappy with Lola.

— Not unhappy, Tony says. I'm bored, really.

— Perhaps it's better to be bored than humiliated.

— It's more than boredom, Tony says. To be honest, I can't stand her. I can't stand that house with a clock in every room and lace curtains on the windows and it's so clean, Alfonso, I didn't know a house could be so clean. It always smells of furniture polish. I don't think I'm a snob, Alfonso, Tony says, but I can't stand Southend-on-Sea. I can't stand the sea there and I can't stand the people and I can't stand the shops. I can't stand the atmosphere. I think I'm going mad.

— No no, Alfonso says. You're not going mad. You just made a mistake.

— I can't go on making mistakes at my age, Tony says. I'm thirty-eight.

— You'll go on making mistakes for a long time to come, believe me, Alfonso says.

— Can't I do something about it?

— Maybe.

— Tell me what.

— If I could I'd be a rich man.

— You're a professor of psychology.

— That's what I mean.

— You're quite rich.

— I'd be very rich.

— Still, Tony says. Tell me what to do.

— I can't do that, Alfonso says. You tell me what *you* plan to do.

— I have to move out, Tony says. I need some space around me. I need to think things through.

— That's wise, Alfonso says. Perhaps you should have thought of that before.

— I know, Tony says. But I've always been with someone.

It didn't seem natural just to move out and be by myself.

He is silent.

— So now you've made two women miserable, Alfonso says.

— Oh, Dot isn't miserable, Tony says. Her pride is wounded but she's probably quite glad to be rid of me.

— You underestimate her feelings for you, Alfonso says.

— She's an independent spirit. She doesn't need anyone.

— You also forget that people may have more than one emotion at the same time. You have always forgotten that.

— I hate myself when I feel I have two conflicting emotions, Tony says.

— Exactly, Alfonso says. That is what is attractive about you. But it is also the source of your unhappiness. He adds: — That is what drew you to Dorothy in the first place. You thought she embodied pure singleness of spirit.

— You think so?

— You told me at the time.

— I did?

— You've forgotten?

— Obviously.

— Oh Tony, Tony, Alfonso says. What are we going to do with you?

— Do you think I'm one of those people who can't live by themselves and can't live with other people? Tony asks.

— Who knows, Alfonso says. That's something you'll have to find out, isn't it?

— You mean by living on my own?

— That, Alfonso says. And time.

— Time?

— Living a bit more. You've not really lived till now, have you?

— How do you mean?

— You've let Dorothy do the living for you.

— I'm still not...?

— You haven't thought about time till now, Alfonso says. Now it will hang heavy on you. It will give you much pain. But it will also give you a chance to come to terms with it.

— I don't know what you're talking about, Tony says.

— Exactly, Alfonso says. But now you are about to find out.

XVII

— I just don't want to go on, Charlie says.

— You can't say that, Angie says.

— Why not?

— You can't.

— I don't think there's any future in it.

— Why not?

— I just don't.

— Don't keep saying that, she says. Give me an explanation.

— Why?

— Why? she says. Don't you think I'm owed an explanation?

— No, he says,

— I gave up Pete for you, she says, I gave up so much. Just for you. And you don't owe me an explanation?

— First of all you didn't give up Pete for a long time, he says.

— What's time got to do with it? she says. I did in the end, didn't I?

— And then I didn't force you to do any of those things.

— You promised you'd leave her.

— I thought I could.

— And now?

— Look, he says, that has nothing to do with it. I just don't want to go on with this.

— Want! she says. All you think about is what you want.

— What else is there? he says. You wouldn't want me if I didn't want you, would you?

She begins to cry. The tears run down her cheeks and into her mouth, leaving lines of mascara and blotches of red on her cheeks and chin. Then she begins to run her nails down her cheeks, screaming with pain as the blood begins to flow.

— Angie! he says. For God's sake, Angie!

She looks at him as though she has never seen him before, then gets up, goes to the cupboard, opens it, takes out a cup and smashes it to the floor. She reaches for another but, leaping up, he grabs her hand. — Angie! he says. Stop that, will you?

— Why? she asks triumphantly. Why?

— Why? he says. Because you're smashing everything up. You're becoming hysterical.

She smiles at him, then holds her bloody fingers up to her eyes. — I want to smash everything up, she says quietly.

— I know, he says. I know. But you'll regret it later.

— There is no later, she says.

— You know you're being hysterical, he says weakly.

— Of course, she says. She smiles at him through her tears. Then she reaches inside the cupboard again, seizes another cup and smashes it to the floor, following it with a glass and then another.

— Angie! he screams. Stop it, will you!

She finds a teapot, examines it as he tries to grab her wrists, then twists away from him and smashes it against the wall.

He sits down at the kitchen table again and watches. She

takes out a pile of plates and lets them fall to the floor. They break and a sliver gashes her leg.

He looks at her, smiling.

She stops. — I want..., she says.

— You want to smash me like the crockery, he says.

— You fucking shithead, she says.

— Don't swear, he says. It upsets me.

— What the fuck do I care if I upset your refined fucking sensibility? she says.

— Angie, he says. Can't we discuss this like rational human beings?

— Fuck you, she says, sitting down and rummaging in the drawer.

— Are you looking for a knife? he asks.

— No. A tissue.

He gets up and finds her one. She bends over and applies it to the gash in her leg.

He watches her in silence.

She gets up, goes to the sink, lets the water run, washes her face. She dries it with the dishcloth.

— Go on, she says. Get out.

— Angie, he says.

— Get the fuck out of here.

He gets up. — I had hoped we could deal with this like civilised human beings, he says.

— Don't give me that shit, she says. Just go. Just go.

He looks round the kitchen. — You don't want me to give you a hand clearing all this up?

She stares at him.

— All right, he says. But I'm sorry it had to end like this.

She goes on staring at him as if she has never seen him before.

— Goodbye, he says.

She stands without moving, staring at him, the dishcloth still in her hand. He has to go round her to get to the door. He opens it and goes out, not looking back, and closes it carefully behind him.

XVIII

— It's good, Tony says. I really like living alone.

— You're not just saying that?

— No, Deirdre, Tony says. I really do. I listen to late Beethoven quartets quite a lot and I feel I'm beginning to face up to all sorts of things I'd never faced up to before.

— You can get up when you want as well, Alfonso says. I find that's the great thing when Deirdre's on one of her jaunts.

— Some of us have to get to an office by nine, Tony says. No matter what's happened to our private lives.

— I keep forgetting, Alfonso says.

— That's a bit hard, Tony says. Not having anyone to talk to in the mornings. Coming home to an empty flat. But once I'm over that I relish it. I really do. And then once a week Sam comes over and I cook for him and we watch something together.

— Who do you listen to, playing Beethoven? Deirdre asks.

— I have the Takács recording, Tony says. I love the way they take the slow movements.

— I hope you'll like this, Deirdre says. It's a recipe I picked up in Tunisia.

— I love everything you do, Tony says. Why do you think I come so often?

— I know, Deirdre says. It's a bit like being an heiress, you never know if people love you for yourself or your food.

— What I feel, Alfonso says, is that we should be grateful to be loved at all, so the reason why we are loved is immaterial.

— I think when something's happened to you such as has happened to me, Tony says, you begin to realise that all this talk about love is so much bunkum.

— I don't think you should generalise from your particular situation, Tony, Deirdre says.

— No no, Tony says. Don't get me wrong. Where would the world be without love? Empty. Of humans at least. But it's a young person's game. After a certain age you are entitled to view it all a little sceptically. This is delicious, by the way.

— Thank you, Deirdre says. I think the lamb could have cooked for another minute.

— We don't need it, Tony says. We jump into it, projecting everything onto some poor person who obviously isn't going to fulfil all our fantasies. And then when they don't we get hurt. It's ridiculous.

— What about sex? Deirdre asks.

— That's the problem, Tony says. But perhaps we shouldn't put it into the same mix as the other. Perhaps our grandfathers were wise. Marriage was a practical and economic transaction, sex was something else.

— For the men, Deirdre says.

— For the men, Tony agrees. For the most part, he adds.

— Of course. But only if you were very rich or very bohemian, Deirdre says.

Tony is busy with his lamb.

— At the weekends, he says, patting his lips with his napkin, I can lie in as long as I like and then spend the day listening to Beethoven if I want. There's a certain pleasure to be had in not talking to a soul. You start to appreciate the silence.

— To my mind the pleasures of solitude have been overdone, Alfonso says. Man is a social animal, after all. Aristotle says a political animal, one who is involved in the *polis* or city.

— But we don't live in Athens any more, Tony says. And when you see what our politicians are like you don't really want to take Aristotle as your model. In the modern world of big cities and virtual reality and instant travel and all the rest of it what is needed is to rediscover the Stoic virtues of self-sufficiency and solitude.

— You know what I like best of all in my travels? Deirdre says. It's the hours by myself on the plane.

— I'm so demanding, Alfonso says.

— You're not demanding at all, Deirdre says, and I wouldn't live with anyone else. But the truth of the matter is we all need solitude and quiet somewhere in our lives.

— But you only enjoy it because you know you've got me to come back to, Alfonso says.

— Of course, she says. Have some more lamb, she says to Tony.

— I couldn't. I'm full.

— There's only sorbet to follow, Deirdre says. And your baklava.

— Only! he protests.

— You're sure you won't have a tiny bit?

— Sure, thanks.

Later, when he has left, Deirdre says: — It's horrible how lonely he is.

— He needs to go through it, Alfonso says.

— You're such a brute, she says.

— He does, you know.

— To teach him a lesson?

— No. To make him find out what he really wants.

— When he began to talk about Beethoven I thought I'd cry, Deirdre says.

— He probably does enjoy listening to him, Alfonso says.

— It made me want to cry, Deirdre says. I never thought I'd hear Tony talk like that.

— I always thought a time might come when he would, Alfonso says.

— You see everything so clearly, she says.

— Maybe.

— We can't let him go on like this, Deirdre says.

— It's all right, Alfonso says. He's not going to kill himself.

— But he's so unhappy.

— We all need a bit of unhappiness in our lives.

— You can speak, she says. You've never had an hour's unhappiness in yours.

— How can you say that so categorically?

— Because I know.

— You're right, he says. And do you know why?

— Of course, she says.

— Because of you, he says.

— But you picked me, she says, because of your nature. And your nature is a happy one.

– Perhaps, he says.

– And it's the same with me, she says.

– Perhaps, he says.

– You see, she says. You always agree with me. That's what makes for mutual happiness.

– Perhaps, he says.

XIX

— I found myself in front of that hat shop the other day, Lionel says to Bea on the balcony in Hans Crescent.

— You mean the one ...?

— Uhuh.

— Did you see her?

— No. I peered in but I couldn't see anyone.

— I'm sure she was around.

— I couldn't see her. I didn't want to go in.

— I don't think Charlie's seeing her any more, she says.

— He isn't?

— No.

— Because you...?

— I don't know. I don't think he is.

He sips his drink. Then he says: — Shall we go indoors?

— I like it here, she says.

— You're not too cold?

— No. It's lovely.

— I rather hoped we might go to bed, he says.

— Oh, she says. Do you mind if we don't for a bit?

— That's all right, he says. Can I give you a little more?

— Thank you, she says, holding up her glass.

They sit in silence.

— Would you mind terribly if we didn't go to bed today? she asks.

— No of course not, he says.

— Good, she says. I feel a bit low today.

— Going to bed might be just the thing then, he says.

— I don't think so, she says.

— Righto, he says.

— You don't mind, do you?

— No no. Of course not.

— Good, she says.

— I saw this rather good film the other day, he says. I can't remember who it was by. Sean Penn was in it. There was this —

— I must go, she says.

— Are you sure?

— Yes, she says.

They sit, listening to the sounds of traffic coming up from the streets below.

She stands up.

— Are you all right? he asks.

— Yes, she says.

In the hall, as he helps her on with her jacket he says: — You won't reconsider?

— Reconsider what?

— Coming to bed with me.

— You're sweet, she says. But no. Not today.

— I haven't done anything...?

— Done?

– I mean offended you or anything?

– How could you think of such a thing? No. It's my fault entirely. I'm sorry.

– Don't apologise.

– I feel bad. I don't know what's the matter with me.

– Don't worry. Another time. When you're feeling better.

– You're sweet. Thank you. And thank you for the drink.

– Goodbye.

– Goodbye, Lionel.

XX

— So, Charlie says, here's to your new life.

— Tell me about your old one, she says.

— There's not much to report, Dot, he says. It trundles on, you know.

— How is my sister?

— She's well.

— They do say the dead are well.

— No. She's very much alive.

— It's ironic, isn't it, she says, the last time I heard from her she was leaving you and coming to find refuge with me and Tony and now it's I who should be coming to you.

— Oh you don't need refuge, Dot, Charlie says. You were always the independent one.

— I suppose if you're the eldest you have to be.

— Besides, he says, we're not much of a refuge, you know.

— What do you mean?

He sips his drink.

— You've given up that woman, I hope, she says.

— What do you know about her?

— Oh, she says, Bea told me everything
— She doesn't know everything.
— Enough, Dorothy says.
— Yes, he says. I've given her up.
— I'm glad, she says.
— Not because of Bea, he says.
— Why then?
— Because of me.
— You?
— She drove me crazy.

— Why do you always go in for such women, Charlie? she asks.

— I don't know, he says. They don't seem crazy at the time. They seem interesting and sexy. Perhaps I drive them crazy.

— No, she says. You pick them like that.

— I picked Bea, he says.

She is silent.

— You, he says.

She is looking down at her glass.

— Perhaps I drove your sister crazy, he says.

She is silent.

— The funny thing, he says, is that I think of myself as the easiest-going guy in the world.

— You are, Charlie, she says.

— You think so, don't you?

— I've just told you.

— Tell me again.

— You're so easygoing no one knows where they stand with you, she says.

— It hurt a lot when you took up with Tony, he says.

— It did?

— Of course.

— I had no idea, she says. I thought you wouldn't mind. You seemed to take our relationship so lightly.

— I never really believed it was happening.

— We were engaged to each other, she says.

— I never really believed you'd want me, he says. In the end.

— I'm sorry, she says.

— Oh, I wasn't angry with you, he says. You and Tony were always made for each other.

— And weren't you and Bea?

— You know it wasn't the same thing.

— Yes, she says. I know.

— Perhaps the expectations were too great with you two, he says.

— Oh no, she says. One must expect everything from life or it's not worth living.

— Oh, wow, he says.

— What's the matter?

— Did you hear yourself, Dot?

— Hear myself?

— One must expect everything from life or it's not worth living.

— So?

— It's unreal, Dot, no one can live like that.

— We did, she says. I do.

— And look where it's got you.

— It hasn't 'got' me anywhere, she says. And I'm very happy where I am.

— Yes, he says. I think you are.

— What's that supposed to mean?

— It means I'm wrong. That you can live like that. But don't expect anyone else to.

— I don't, she says.

— Tony obviously thought you did.

— That's his problem, she says.

— I couldn't agree with you more, he says.

— Now he's left his secretary and is living on his own in a room Alfonso found him, she says, he wants me to think again about the divorce but I told him it's out of the question.

— I heard, he says.

— How?

— Bea bumped into Alfonso. He told her.

— I see.

— You're not concerned for him?

— Of course I am, she says. He's not made to live on his own. He can't handle it. He thinks he can but he can't.

He is silent.

— I'm not his keeper, though, she says.

— No no. Of course not.

— He's got to face up to things, she says.

— He sees Sam?

— Of course. But he's so hopeless. We fix a time and then he rings up and says he can't. Or else he won't bring him back when I want him.

— These things are difficult, he says.

— Other people seem to sort them out.

— I wonder, he says.

— I just want a bit of co-operation, she says. It's not too much to ask.

— I'm sure he thinks he's co-operating, he says.

— Why are you taking his side all the time? she asks.

— In the interest of fair play, he says, laughing.

— No you're not, she says. You do it to contradict.

— You're right, he says. I love contradicting you. I'd forgotten how much fun it was.

— Why?

— Why had I forgotten?

— No. Why do you love it?

— Because you ask wide-eyed questions like that.

— Wide-eyed? she says. What are you talking about?

— You are funny, Dot, he says.

— No one ever says that about me, she says.

— To me you are, he says.

XXI

— What have you done to your beard? Tony asks as soon as Alfonso opens the door.

— Don't you like it? Alfonso asks.

— Have you dyed it or what?

— Dyed it, Alfonso confesses.

— It looks splendid anyway, Tony says, handing him his coat.

— It was either that, Alfonso says, or shaving it off.

— Perish the thought! Tony says.

— We've asked someone you know, Alfonso says, showing his white teeth in a smile as he stands back to allow Tony through into the living-room.

— Good heavens! Tony says.

— Hullo! Beatrice says.

Tony kisses Deirdre and then his sister-in-law.

— I heard you commenting on his beard, Deirdre says.

— I couldn't quite see what he'd done at first, Tony says. Only that there was something very splendid about his face.

— There were too many white hairs beginning to show

through, Alfonso says.

— Do you like it? Deirdre asks.

— Do you?

— Oh yes, she says.

— I'm not sure, Tony says.

— Why?

— I don't know. It looks... manured.

They laugh.

— I mean, he says, it draws attention to itself. One feels the need to comment on it. If that's what you want...

— It's just because you were used to the old look, Alfonso says.

— But you've cut it differently?

— No. It's just as it always was.

— So it's just the dye...?

— Uhuh.

— What do you think? Deirdre asks Bea.

— I don't know, Bea says. It's certainly striking.

— I suppose manured is a good word, Alfonso says. One's beard is a bit like one's garden. Something both outside and inside one's private space, to be tended or not as one wishes, allowed to flourish or cut ruthlessly down. One can employ a person to prune it or one can do it oneself. One can take pride in it or treat it as a necessary evil. I can see a whole new genre of gardening-cum-beard books, the small-town beard, the cottage beard, the country beard, the Mediterranean, English, Himalayan beard, who knows, we might even have mystic Japanese stone beards. What do you think?

— You're all going to be guinea-pigs tonight, Deirdre says. I've been trying out a few recipes I learned about on my recent trip to Samarkand.

— I didn't know you had kept up with these people, Tony says to Beatrice as they sit down at the table.

— I hadn't, she says. But I met Alfonso on the tube and he took my number and here I am.

— *I* met you on the tube, Tony says. But I forgot to take your number.

— You had other things on your mind, Bea says.

— Do you take the tube a great deal? Deirdre asks.

— Not really, Bea says. I always feel it's a good sign when one meets people one knows in the middle of London.

— Why? Alfonso asks.

— Because the chances of its happening are so small in a city this size. So it's a sign that fortune hasn't entirely abandoned you.

— Fortune? Alfonso asks. Or God?

— No no, Bea says. I don't believe in God.

— But you believe in fortune?

— You have to, she says. If things like that happen.

— You haven't considered chance? he asks.

— That kind of chance I call fortune, she says.

— Destiny? asks Deirdre, putting mysterious things onto their plates. You have to swallow these down and then I'll give you another version with a little more cumin, she says.

— No, Beatrice says. Destiny is too big a word.

— I like that, Tony says to Deirdre.

— Now try this one.

He does so.

— Well? she says.

— I think I prefer the first.

— Bea?

— Yes, the first.

— A little too doughy, Alfonso says.

— The first or the second?

— Both.

— It has to be doughy.

— A little too much for my taste.

— That's why I never take him with me, Deirdre says. He has reservations about everything.

— You wouldn't want me to be a yes-man, would you?

— There's a balance, she says.

— Definitely the first, Tony says.

— I think I prefer the second, Alfonso says.

— No more tests till the dessert, Deirdre says. There's only the main course.

— And may one ask what that is? Tony asks,

— No, she says. One must wait.

— Ouch, Tony says.

— It's Nile perch if you want to know.

— Nile perch? I've never heard of that.

— It's not easy to find in England.

— Are there any other kinds of perch?

— Oh, it's a common British and European dark freshwater fish. There's an American yellow perch that's very common too.

— My ignorance is abysmal, Tony says.

— Don't apologise, Alfonso says. Why should you know anything about fish? Do you think she knows anything about banking?

— Why should one know anything about anything?

— I've always liked that bit in Sherlock Holmes, Alfonso says, where Watson explains to a puzzled Holmes that the earth goes round the sun, and Holmes says: 'Very interesting, Watson. Now I know this I shall endeavour to forget it.' And when asked why he explains that he thinks of the brain as a metal box that tends to get so full that if you add one more object to it another has to be pushed out to make way for it. Now though I know perfectly well that that is not how the brain works it feels intuitively right to me.

He strokes his now red beard and smiles at them.

— Here comes the perch of the Nile, Deirdre says. Can you clear a space on the table?

XXII

Charlie and Dorothy are walking along the beach in Brighton.

— So he begins to spend more and more time in the bathroom, Charlie says. No explanation is given, but it's clear that he just likes it better like that. He lies in the empty tub fully clothed and listens to the radio. Or daydreams. Sometimes his girlfriend comes in, sits on the lavatory and tells him what she's been up to at the gallery where she works. Her name is Edmondsson, so at first one thinks it must be a man and then it —

— Be quiet, Dorothy says.

He stops.

— I'm sorry, she says. I'm not listening to you. I want to take all this in.

— That's all right, he says.

— Can we sit for a moment?

— Of course.

They sit on the shingle.

— I do go on, he says. I don't know why.

They look at the copper sea.

— It's crazy, she says. What did it take us? A couple of hours? And it's a different world.

They gaze out at the water.

— I love it so much when I come to a place like this, she says. Yet somehow I don't ever think of doing it by myself.

— I thought you might enjoy it, he says.

She lies back on the shingle, looking up into the cloudless sky. He sits beside her, playing with a stone.

— Listen to the tide, she says.

— That's why I like shingle beaches, he says. The Mediterranean's wonderful but you don't have this sound of the tide sucking in the shingle and then letting it out, sucking it in and letting it out.

They listen.

— It's more than just a regular sound, he says. It's like the world breathing. In. Out. In. Out. In. Out.

— That's why it's so restorative, she says. It brings you back to something basic inside you. That cities make you forget.

They listen.

— Everything seems to drain away from you, she says. All the worries. The anxieties. Just drains away.

— It's typical of Arnold that he would have allegorised this, he says. The one thing one doesn't want to do is allegorise it. When he —

She lays a hand on his arm: — Please.

— I'm sorry.

— I just want to listen.

— Of course. I talk too much.

— Shshshshshsh.

He looks down at her hand on his arm. After a while she

lets it fall back onto the shingle.

He lies down beside her, closes his eyes.

Later, when he opens his eyes, she is sitting up beside him, looking out at the sea.

He examines the sky, streaked now with pale pink and grey clouds.

She turns and looks down at him.

He smiles at her. — I slept, he says.

— Like a baby, she says.

He puts his hand on hers. — You're cold, he says.

— No, she says. Not really.

She does not withdraw her hand.

— What would you like to do? he asks her.

— Shshshshsh, she says.

— I didn't mean —

— Shshshshshsh, she says again. Don't always be thinking of what you're going to do.

— It's my nature, he says.

— Curb it.

He sighs.

— Go on, she says, laughing. Do what you like.

— No, he says. I don't mind.

He sits up, rubbing his face. — How long did I sleep for? he asks.

— Hours, she says.

— Hours?

— Half an hour.

He looks at his watch: — Is that all?

— You were right out, she says.

— I was?

— Right out.

– Oh dear.

– Why oh dear? It's good.

– I must have been feeling at ease.

– That's good.

– Shall we make a move?

– Let me ring Sam.

When she has finished he says: – It's all right?

– Yes. Fine. Do you know what Tony said to me the other day?

– What?

He said: – You wanted me to be the sort of husband you expected to have and now you want me to be just the sort of separated father you expect your child to have.

He stands up. – Come, he says.

He reaches out his hand. She takes it and stands up. She withdraws her hand.

– That's not fair, is it? she says, as they start to walk.

They walk.

On the drive back she says: – I can't get the sound of the sea out of my head.

– Me too, he says.

– I'm breathing differently, she says.

And then, later: – Thank you.

– For what?

– For taking me.

– We went together, he says.

– You suggested it.

– That's true, he says. I'm good at suggestions.

XXIII

Tony and Bea are strolling round Kew Gardens. Tony had said: — If it rains we can always go into one of the greenhouses. But it's not raining. It's a bright and balmy spring day.

— It must have been hard for you, Tony says, with Charlie wandering like that.

— I haven't been squeaky clean myself, Beatrice says.

— Really? he says. He looks at her: — You surprise me, he says.

— Do I? she says, laughing. You're such an idealist, Tony, she says.

They walk.

— Besides, she says, we suited each other. We found a way of living.

— And the children?

— They have to learn about life too, don't they?

— Yes, but...

— They know we love them. That's the main thing.

They reach the lake and stand, looking at the ducks and coots.

– I suppose you're right, he says. But I've always felt –

– I'm not right, she says. You're the one who's right. But that's how it's worked out.

– Do you want to sit? he asks.

– All right.

They find a bench.

– Or not, she says as they sit down.

– Not what?

– Not worked out.

He is silent.

– But then what does 'worked out' mean anyway? she says.

He is silent.

– Everything 'works out' she says. Only not in the way one was expecting.

He is silent.

– Not that I ever expected very much, she says.

He is silent.

After a while he says: – I did.

– I know, she says.

– How do you know?

– That's how you are, she says. And Dot.

– Yes, he says. She expects a great deal.

– Everything, she says, she always expected everything. And would never settle for less.

– And you? he asks.

– Me? She laughs. I picked up the crumbs, she says.

– Oh come on!

– I like crumbs, she says. Don't get me wrong. Whole slices of cake are too rich for me.

– Don't run yourself down.

– I'm not. Perhaps some of us are like sparrows. We're wired to live on crumbs mixed with dirt.

– Bea, he says, I want to talk to you.

– You are talking to me.

– Not about cakes and crumbs, he says.

– That's only one of the things we've been talking about, she says.

– Stop, he says Let me speak.

– Speak away, she says.

– It's difficult, he says.

She waits.

– I've been thinking a lot, he says. Since I started to live on my own. Perhaps we all made a mistake. All those years ago. Me especially, what do you think?

– I don't know.

– Tell me what you think.

– Perhaps, she says.

– Do you remember the first time we saw each other?

– Of course, she says. How could I forget?

– How could you forget, he says. Indeed. It was in the Parks. You were doing a headstand in the grass. I was walking on the path and I stopped and looked.

– Stared, she says.

– I couldn't believe what I was seeing, he says. Here was this girl. Upside down. With her eyes closed. Concentrating, I suppose. And then you opened them and our gazes met.

– Yes, she says.

– You didn't blink, he says. You kept your position.

– I was curious to see how long it would be before you turned away, she says.

— I didn't.

— No, she says. You kept staring at me. So I stuck my tongue out at you. And then you blushed and walked on.

— I was embarrassed, he says. As if I shouldn't have been looking. As if you'd been naked or something.

She is silent.

— And then that evening I went to a party, he says, and met Dorothy and we danced a lot and she took me back to her flat. She told me to be quiet because her sister was staying from Bristol. And the next morning at breakfast there you were. Right side up.

— I didn't realise for a moment or two that you were the one, she says. I too had only seen you wrong side up.

— I recognised you at once, he says.

— I know, she says. You told me.

— We couldn't stop looking at each other, he says.

— Dot didn't know what was going on, she says.

— We explained to her, he says. She didn't seem to understand. And then we left her and went out together.

— You asked me if I always stood on my head in the Parks, she says. And I said yes. And then later that day you introduced Charlie to Dot and they started going out. And then Alfonso played that silly trick on us. And then you came round and told me you'd made a big mistake and it was Dot you'd been in love with all along.

— Yes, he says.

— That it wasn't for nothing that you'd danced with her all night.

— No.

— But that was obvious from the start, she says. I was waiting for it to happen.

— You were?

— All the time. But that didn't make it any less painful when it did, she says.

— No, he says. I can see that.

They sit.

— Before that, he says. Before I told you. When I went down to Devon to think things through. I had begun to feel that perhaps we had built too much on that first encounter. That I at any rate had been behaving like a romantic adolescent. That I'd been obsessed by the image of you standing on your head and then sticking your tongue out at me. It seemed like a portent at the time. As if that somehow sealed a pact between the two of us. But, I thought, perhaps it's nothing of the sort. If I'd come along five minutes later you'd have been upright again. Or no longer there. And, after all, I'd been drawn to Dorothy at the party and she was the one I'd slept with first, and something of that had been reawakened when we spent the weekend together, though both of us felt guilty as hell at what we were doing. But as I thought about things, walking on the cliffs in Devon, it became clear to me that I had to free myself from the image of you as I'd first seen you. I had to face the fact that perhaps I'd made a terrible mistake and drawn everyone else into it.

— You didn't draw everyone in, she says. We were all to blame. And anyway Charlie and I were much more suited to each other really.

— Were you? he asks.

— Of course, she says.

They sit.

— You don't believe that, he says.

— I don't know, she says.

— And now I want to say something else, he says. I've been

thinking a lot since I've been living on my own. And I think now that perhaps I was right in the first place. Of course I was attracted to Dot. Of course I admired her. Who wouldn't? But perhaps my initial instinct was right. It was only the rationalisation that was wrong. Perhaps it wasn't an image of you I was drawn to but you. Because in that first moment I saw who you were. Much more clearly than if you had in fact been naked. And who I was, too. Do you now what I mean?

She is silent.

— What do you think? he asks.

— You mean second thoughts are always a mistake? she asks.

He laughs. — I think often, yes. First thoughts are perhaps more to be trusted than second.

— And third?

He is silent. Then he says: — Would you consider trying again?

— Are you proposing to me? she asks.

— I suppose I am, he says.

— Bigamist.

— We're both of us bigamists, he says. If you stick to the letter of the law.

She is silent.

— Well? he says.

— Why don't you try kissing me? she says. If I slap you you'll know the answer.

— Here?

She begins to laugh.

— It's difficult, he says. Now you've put it like that.

— Oh, Tony! she says. And to think I was once in awe of you.

— Of me?

– Of course.

– And you thought only your sister was worthy of me?

– Uhuh.

– You did or you didn't?

– Of course I did.

– Let's go behind those bushes, he says. Then we can try our little experiment.

He gets up.

– Come, he says, holding out his hand to her.

She takes his hand and stands up. Then she puts her arms round his neck and presses her lips to his.

XXIV

— Have you done something to your beard? Nigel asks as he enters the room.

— He's dyed it, Deirdre says.

— I don't believe it, Henrietta says.

— Why not? Alfonso says. I was beginning to see the white hairs in it.

— I've heard of people waxing their moustaches, Henrietta says, but I've never heard of anyone dying their beards. And that colour!

— You don't think it makes it look more… luxuriant? Deirdre says.

— Luxuriant?

— Yes.

— I suppose…

— You don't think it's more luxuriant?

— I had a friend, Tony says, who became obsessed with his allotment. He'd go up and work on it in any spare time he had. One day, when the circus was in town, he saw an advert for elephant manure. They were giving it away to anyone willing to cart it away. So he went and got a sack or two and laid it down. And do you know, he told me later, everything I'd laid that manure on grew three times faster and three times larger than it ever had before.

— What are you trying to say? Henrietta asks him.

— I'm trying to say, Tony says, that I suspect Alfonso here's not only dyed his beard, but soaks it regularly in elephant dung. It's the most luxurious I've ever seen it.

— That's a disgusting thought, Henrietta says.

— Why? Bea asks. There's nothing wrong with dung, is there?

— Not with dung as such, Henrietta says, but the idea of soaking your beard in it...!

— People put all sorts of things on their faces, Beatrice says. It's a matter of habit. Of convention.

— Not everything's convention, Henrietta says. Look at incest for instance.

— I think you'd find the anthropologists against you there, Deirdre says.

— I don't intend to dye it for ever, Alfonso says. I look forward to a time when I have a long white beard. But it has to be all white.

— Politeness, Henrietta says. Every society has its own norms of politeness, but every society has a concept of it.

— But that's exactly it, Deirdre says. Its own norms. Some people find it polite to say nothing and others find it rude, some find it polite to refuse something that's offered to you, others rude. And so on. Even gestures are conventional. Europeans nod to say yes —

— And Turks nod to say no, Henrietta says. But that's not the point I was trying to make.

— Could you sleep with a man with a beard? Nigel asks Bea.

— Why? she says.

— I just wondered. I wondered how women felt about beards.

— I can't speak for women, Bea says.

— But what about you?

— It would depend on the man.

— Not on the beard?

— Well…

— Would the beard be a *factor*?

— Everything's a factor, Bea says.

— What about discovering it was dyed?

— That might be more of a problem, Bea says.

— Would you feel you'd been lied to?

— Not lied to, no.

— What then?

— You're going to have to be guinea-pigs tonight, Deirdre announces. I'm trying out some different recipes given me on my recent visit to Goa.

— You've been to Goa? Was it official? Henrietta says.

— Are you regaling us with Portuguese or with Chinese dishes tonight? Nigel asks.

— It's a bi-annual food-fest, Deirdre says.

— Did you go? Henrietta asks Alfonso.

— I never go to those things, Alfonso says. I prefer my steak and kidney pie here in London,

— I never knew you liked steak and kidney pie, Nigel says.

— Don't listen to him, Deirdre says.

— Is he lying through his teeth again?

— I've never made this before, Deirdre says at the oven, so you'll have to be indulgent.

– I can't wait, Nigel says. Can you? he asks Bea.

– No, she says.

– I always feel it's such a privilege to be asked to dinner here, Nigel says.

– It is, isn't it? she says.

The phone rings.

– I'll take it, Alfonso says.

He leaves the room with the phone at his ear.

– Have you been to Goa? Henrietta asks Tony.

– No, he says. Have you?

– I've always wanted to go, she says. Ever since I saw a film about it. Those pink houses. And the beaches. It looked so amazing.

Alfonso returns. He replaces the phone in its cradle and slides in between Beatrice and Henrietta.

– We're starting with some little things I learned about in Acapulco last year, Deirdre says.

– It's a privilege to be here, Nigel says.

– You haven't tasted them yet, Deirdre says.

– Just being a guinea-pig, Nigel says.

– That was your sister, Alfonso says to Beatrice.

Her face goes white: – Dot?

– I told her you were here. She sends her love. They're just off to Hawaii.

– Hawaii?

– A little celebratory holiday. We saw them the other day. They seem very happy.

– Really?

– Absolutely.

– I'm glad.

– So am I, Alfonso says, stroking his luxuriant beard. You

know, Bea, he says, I always felt this would be the outcome.

— You didn't?

— I sort of felt it, yes.

— *I* didn't.

— No, he says. Of course not. You were in the middle of it. How could you?

— It would have saved a lot of heartache, she says.

— I don't know, he says. Heartache's a pretty constant factor in human life. And think of all those beautiful children who would never have come into the world.

— One can't think like that, she says. It's crazy.

— That's exactly how one has to think, he says.

— That's sort of everything's the best in the best of all possible worlds sort of thing.

— No. It just recognises that what is, is.

— And this is?

— Indubitably.

— The past and the present?

— And the two of us talking, here.

— But what about your beard? Is it red or speckled?

— You always liked to tease me, Bea, he says.

— No. I like to sort out the logic of things.

— Take your places, Deirdre says. Just eat a bit of everything and then give me your views.

— It's a privilege being here, Nigel says. It really is.

XXV

— Can I interest you in some gloves? the assistant asks.

— I don't think so, Lionel says. It was just the hat I was after.

— We have some very nice pigskin gloves that have only just come in from Ireland, she says. You're sure you don't want to try them on?

— You think I should?

— What do you lose?

— Time? he suggests.

She brushes it aside. — Don't speak about time in this shop.

— It exists outside time? he asks, intrigued.

— Of course, she says.

He looks into her large grey eyes beneath the golden fringe.

— Let me see them.

She pulls out boxes, lays them on the glass counter.

— One never grows old, working here? he asks.

She laughs. — Never, she says.

— Here, she says, try these on. They will go with the hat.

She smoothes them down over his fingers. — Feel it, she says. Isn't it soft?

— What do you do? he asks, holding his hand up to the light. When you're not working here?

— I'm writing a Ph.D, she says. On Poussin.

— The painter?

— Is there another?

— I don't know, he says, confused.

He turns his hand about, encased in the soft leather.

— How does it feel? she asks.

— Nice, he says.

— Try these, she says, holding out a lighter pair. Here, she says, let me help you take them off.

— What aspect of Poussin? he ventures to ask.

— I call it 'Eden and Paradise in the work of Nicolas Poussin', she says.

— Aren't they the same thing?

— Oh no! she says. Eden is the world before the Fall, but it is a world on this earth, that we can perhaps return to. Paradise is the realm of the gods and we can only get there after death.

— I see, he says. And which do you prefer?

— It's not a question of preferring, Angie says. It's a question of exploring the meaning the two concepts had for Poussin and how this is reflected in his work.

— And how is it reflected in his work?

— That's a lecture on Poussin, she says, laughing. You have to pay extra for that.

— I can pay, he says, smiling at her.

— It's quite a lot of money, she says.

— Why don't you come round to my place for tea one of these days? he says. We can sit on the balcony overlooking the square and you can give me your lecture on Poussin.

— Oh, it costs more than a cup of tea, she says.

— How much?

— I'll have to think about it, she says. There's a sliding scale. It depends on what you can afford.

— All the more reason to come to tea, he says. Then you can see where I stand on the scale.

He feels her gaze resting his face. — Here, he says, pulling out a card. Here's my address. Would next Saturday at four be good for you?

— I can't on Saturday, she says. What about Sunday?

— Sunday is fine, he says. Four o'clock.

— Why are you so keen on four o'clock? she asks.

— I'm not! he protests. I just thought you'd like me to suggest a time.

— Can I come at five past four?

— Come at five, he says.

— No. Five past four will be fine, she says. — And these? she asks, pointing to the gloves?

— I'll take the darker pair.

— They go well with the hat, she says.

Expertly, she makes a parcel of his purchases.

— Are you a painter yourself? he asks.

— No. Why?

— You have a painter's hands.

— Do I?

— Absolutely.

— No, she says. I only think about paintings.

— Why only? he says, handing her his credit card. There are enough paintings in the world already and perhaps not enough thought has been given to them.

She accompanies him to the door.

— I'll see you on Sunday then, he says. It's just behind Harrods.

— Five past four, she says.

— No no, he says, laughing. Come when you want,

— I am very precise, she says. You'll see, I'll be there at five past four.

— Do you want us to synchronise our watches? he asks.

She opens the door for him. — *À bientôt*, she says.

— *À bientôt*, he responds.